THE SUNNYSIDE STORY

THE SUNNYSIDE STORY

To: Wet

All The Best

Ora Martin 9-1-21

ORA TANNER-MARTIN

THE SUNNYSIDE STORY

CONTENTS

DEDICATION

On behalf of my siblings and I, I would like to express our love and gratitude for our parents, Willie and Ora Tanner, for raising us to be who we are today. We are thankful to you for every sacrifice and every lesson that you instilled in us since we were young. We will be forever grateful to God for the time He allowed us to share with you. This book, which holds all of the beautiful memories and history of our lives, is dedicated to you, our parents.

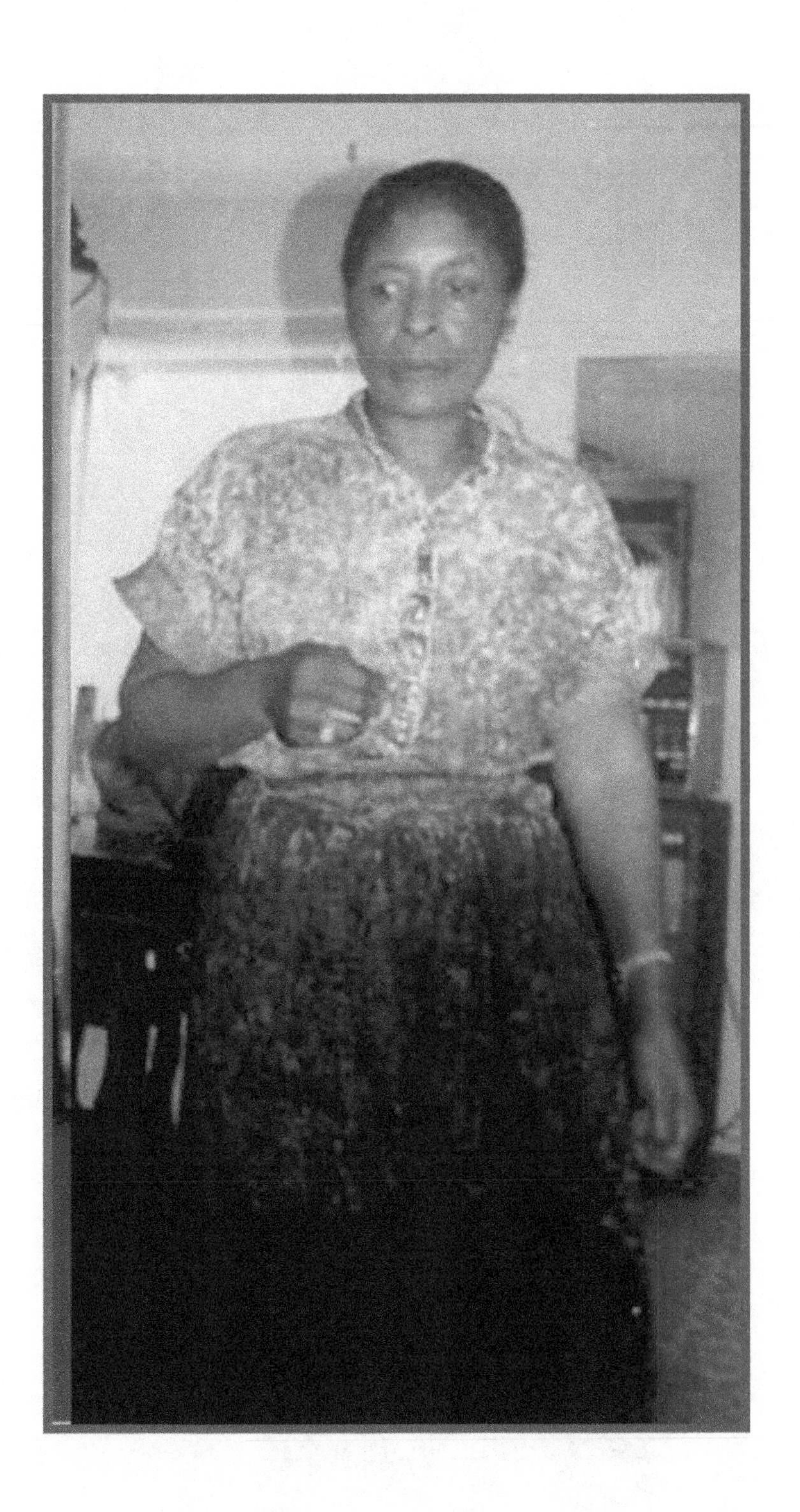

CHAPTER 1

WELCOME TO MISSISSIPPI

Sunnyside, Mississippi was a well-known rural area located between Minter City and Schlater, Mississippi. About seventeen miles from Sunnyside was Greenwood. I was raised in Sunnyside in the 1950s. Back then, only about one-hundred seventy-five people lived in Sunnyside, most of them black.

I was born to Willie and Ora Tanner, the third of seven children. Growing up in a small, southern area in Mississippi didn't take long for me to realize the effects that racism and poverty would have on my experiences.

As a young child, I didn't understand the significance of not having food and clothes or what it took to make ends meet for a family of nine. I didn't understand or even have a clue of just how hard our parents had to work to provide for us. The struggles and strains of poverty undoubtedly took a major emotional toll on our parents, but it wasn't until I got a little older that I truly began to understand the severity of their struggle.

There were many times we didn't have good shoes to wear. Some of our shoes had holes in the soles, but we had to wear them anyway. Momma would put cardboard in the bottom of our shoes, trying to keep our feet from getting wet when it rained. It was seven of us, and it was hard trying to keep clothes and shoes for all of us. We missed many days of school because we didn't have decent clothes and shoes to wear. During some winters, we didn't even have sufficient coats to wear.

If bearing the weight of poverty wasn't enough, racism and prejudice seemed to plague every aspect of our life in Sunnyside, especially on the plantations. I watched grown men and women being handled like small, untrained children, even my parents by white landowners. My parents worked Mr. Bill's land. I remember the attitude and tone of Mr. Bill's voice as he would talk to my parents and other workers.

Black people worked as tenant farmers. The work done on plantations was just a fragment of a culture that was rooted in slavery, evident in the way black workers and white landowners interacted with one another. Even as children, we recognized the air of racism that loomed around each and every interaction we had with Mr. Bill and other landowners.

Whenever Mr. Bill spoke to our parents, any message that he would give was for our entire family, including me, my brothers and sisters. My parents were expected to relay the message back to us. I remember Mr. Bill always wanting us to go pick berries, shell peas, or pick cucumbers for his wife. He would tell our parents of her requests;

we'd be off to fulfill them. Sometimes older children would steal from Mr. Bill, so to keep me and my siblings from getting in trouble, Mr. Bill would tell our parents to make sure we weren't on his property.

If for any reason my parents didn't get the message across to us in time, Mr. Bill was given the right to handle the trespassers in his own way, and that went for us and any other child that found himself on Mr. Bill's property.

One night, I remember Mr. Bill chasing some teenage boys off of his land after he found them stealing gas out of his tractors, shooting at them from his small pick-up truck. Even though those boys could outrun Mr. Bill's truck, I don't think they considered having to outrun Mr. Bill's bullets. He chased them as far as he could, but once they made it into the corn field, it was over. Mr. Bill soon gave up, unable to drive his truck across the corn field.

In the country, stealing gas was so common; it may as well have been a tradition. Hardly anyone actually bought gas. Young guys usually stole gas to put in their parent's cars in order to go dating.

"Now I bet' not catch y'all messin' 'round on Mr. Bill's land," Momma would warn us, pointing her crooked finger in our face and perching her lips with one eye closed. If Momma pointed that crooked fingers and closed that one eye, we knew she meant business.

My siblings and I never had an issue with Mr. Bill for sneaking on his land. After all, being caught by Mr. Bill would've been the least of our problems. Getting caught by Momma would've been a whole different story.

Momma was always protective of us, especially when it came to Mr. Bill. She tried her hardest to get us in order so that Mr. Bill never had a reason to. Watching how Mr. Bill talked to the other workers made us nervous and afraid, so I thank God for our parents for keeping us close to them.

Since as long as I can remember, our parents had to work in the fields, chopping cotton with cotton stalks standing tall as trees while the glaring sun had no mercy on field hands. Momma and Daddy worked hard in the fields, doing all that they could do to provide for us, and when my siblings and I got old enough, we worked alongside them. In the summer, sweat poured down our faces like rain and landowners watched over us from the time the workday began until the very end.

I can still remember working in the brutal summer sun, sunrays beating down on our backs, skin burned and lips parched because of the limited access to water we had while working in the fields. Sometimes, we had to wait for hours for Mr. Bill to bring water out to the fields. In the winter, our fingers would be so cold that we could hardly bend them to pick the next lock of cotton.

Mississippi was marked as the most repressive states in the south because of the cruelty and violence that black people experienced during and following the end of slavery. We didn't go through the same racial terror most of our ancestors faced, but we had our share of hard times. I still remember Mr. Bill beating an older black man because he came to work a few minutes late. He never asked him why he was late, just began screaming, cursing and punching the poor man until he fell to the ground. When he fell to the ground, Mr. Bill began kicking, eventually growing tired.

"Now, I expect you to be finished choppin' this field 'thin the next hour," he'd growl, as he walked across the fields, with a cigar hanging from his mouth and straw hat flopped down on his head.

He'd make his way through each row, and if the work that had been completed was to his liking, he'd return to his truck and leave, but the work was almost never to his liking.

Mr. Bill was as mean as a bulldog. He talked with a deep tone, and if you listened closely, you could almost hear the hate in his voice.

"Get your behind over here!"

The way Mr. Bill barked orders at the workers made my blood boil. Sometimes I would get so upset that it felt like flames would shoot from my ears. I never said anything to Mr. Bill, or anyone else for that matter, but one thing I did was listen.

"When you done here, gon' on and start on that next one," he'd say, the bottom of his lip filled with chewing tobacco.

No one ever responded to Mr. Bill's orders with the same tone he spoke to them, but as soon as he was out of earshot, everyone had a word or two.

Momma always kept us close to her when we'd go to work in the fields, so every chance I got, I listened to the talks that Momma and the other women had amongst themselves. Usually, they talked about things that had happened on the plantation or, complained about the way Mr. Bill talked to them. Even though nothing was said to Mr. Bill, the talks they had with one another seemed like it helped them lighten the burdens that hung over them like storm clouds. They surely passed the time more quickly.

I couldn't wait for those women to start talking. It usually took them a minute to get the conversation going after Mr. Bill left the field. When everyone was in place and the children were in position to start working, the women would start their talking periodically glancing over their shoulders to make sure Mr. Bill was nowhere to be found.

"I'm tired of the way that man been treatin' us. He don't do nothin' but ride 'round in dat truck bossin' us 'round," one would burst out.

"Then he don't even pay us half what he owe us mos' the time," another would respond.

There were plenty of times when Mr. Bill cheated the workers out of their pay or made them wait until late Saturday afternoon to get paid after working hard all week long.

Even in the midst of their complaints, someone would always try to shed light on their situation.

"Time gon' bring about change. Thangs ain'tgon' stay the same forever. Better days soon to come," she'd say, "Honey, God knows, and he sees it all, and in due time, he gonna fix it."

At times the women would talk in a round-about way, not saying what they really meant. They were careful with their words, depending on who was working alongside them. There were always snitches, and what Momma would call "snakes in the grass," running back and telling Mr. Bill what was said.

"Well, if a change don't hurry up and come, somebody gon' die," one of the women would say, as she made her way through the rows of cotton to take a spit break.

Life wasn't easy living on plantations and working for harsh landowners, and poverty did nothing but agitated the already unfavorable circumstances that we experienced every day.

Witnessing the pain that my family endured, I can only imagine the troubles that other workers faced that I'm sure had the power to swallow them whole but thank God for always redeeming their brokenness.

When we became older, our parents would often sit us down and have family talks, sharing with us the facts of life. They mostly talked about how difficult it was trying to feed and keep a roof over our heads, but occasionally they would explain how their inability to take themselves or us, their children, to the doctor when we got sick took an emotional toll on them as our parents. I would sometimes see Momma with tears in her eyes because we didn't have food or money to meet all of our household needs, nor did we have anyone to call for help.

When I was fourteen, Momma talked to me even more about her problems. Sometimes she'd try to shy away from the conversation, but I would do all that I could to make her open up.

"Even after this week's pay, I don't have enough money left to buy food for the week," I remember Momma expressing to me one day while counting a handful of dollars that she and Daddy kept in a box underneath the bed.

"So, what are you going to do?" I asked, hoping to continue, treasuring every moment of our talks.

But, as soon as Momma noticed me getting too inquisitive, she retreated.

"Gal, you gettin' a little too wommanish," she'd say, rubbing me on my cheek, a polite way of telling me to shut up and stop asking so many questions.

I wasn't trying to be nosey, as Momma probably thought, but I wanted to know what I could do to make it easier on her, and on my family.

Though my parents began to speak to us more and more about the struggles they faced the older we got, they decided that some things were not for them to share with us. So, Momma would go over to the neighbor's house and talk to them, Mr. and Mrs. Johnson.

Desperate to know the unknown, I often found myself snooping around the front porch of the Johnson's home to hear even a word of the conversation shared between Momma and Mrs. Johnson. Despite my fear of snakes, I'd crawl underneath the porch and listen. After some time, others would join them. It was always the same women, Ms. Ethel, Mrs. Freeman, and Lottie Mae, who lived across the road from us.

Those little country women could talk some real trash.

"If he don't be careful," Momma would say, "I'm liable to cut that man new butt hole."

The women would cackle like hens as they went around the group talking about Mr. Bill. They found laughter in one another's company sharing their hate for Mr. Bill and their aggravation with their working conditions, but they never stopped working as they laughed and talked about Mr. Bill.

Sometimes, Mr. Bill showed favoritism toward certain workers, allowing them to work the fields with less grass and weeds. He always looked for a reason to scold the workers he didn't care for, whether it be for working too slow and not getting as much done as other workers or working too fast and not picking all the cotton from a bush.

Mommy and Daddy weren't the only ones tired of not being able to get the things that we needed and wanted. Still, no matter how many of us worked and how hard we worked, it seemed like the less we earned.

The gloom of growing up poor, working in the scorching heat or the freezing cold, never having enough to live comfortably took a toll on us all, but somehow, our parents always found a way of sustaining our family through difficult times. In the desperate circum-stances, we learned how to be strong and resilient, to be grateful for the little we did have. They showed us that no matter what obstacles we faced, we could overcome.

CHAPTER 2

GROWING UP IN SUNNYSIDE MISSISSIPPI

Seing that Sunnyside was so small, everyone knew what was going in everyone's personal lives. We knew the families dealing with marriage problems and who was cheating on who. All night long, you could hear men walking the roads creeping and sneaking into single women's homes. Married couples had more children outside of their marriages than they had at home. In the country, everybody was related in some way because there was so much sleeping around.

Even though we heard of everything that happened, but as children, you didn't and wouldn't dare to question your parents about grown folks' personal business. If you heard them talking about Ms. Sally not having groceries, or Mr. Ben jumping on his wife, or the Smith family losing their car, you knew better than to ask them anything more about it. If they didn't tell us we most definitely didn't ask them. Everything they talked about was "grown folk business." We knew when our parents said that some information was "grown folk business" it was time for us to go sit down and shut up.

There were times I would hear my parent's and neighbors talking about things that had taken place from time to time in other families or on the other plantations. Many issues were swept under the rug. Not one person had the guts to say that they saw Mr. Strong, another white landowner, or Mr. Watts sneaking around people's homes at night trying to catch the husband or boyfriend gone.

It was usually on Saturday nights when white men would try to invade black women's privacy when they knew that most black men would be at the juke joints drinking and partying. Most black women were too afraid to say anything about the white landowners sneaking into black men's houses and sleeping with their wives or daughters.

White men raping and impregnating black women was common in the south. Women were unable to fight, and men lacked the courage to confront their white bosses out of fear of being beaten and even killed; so, everyone suffered in silence.

Women weren't the only people who fell victim to the attacks of white men.

Only two miles away from Sunnyside was Money, Mississippi. If no one had heard of Money before, in 1955, everyone knew about Money. That year, Emmet Till, a fourteen-year-old black boy from Chicago, Illinois had come down to Money to visit his uncle.

After being accused of making sexual advances at a white woman in a grocery store, Emmett was abducted by a gang of white men, taken to a shed and brutally beaten, shot, and drowned in the Tallahatchie River.

I was only four years old when Emmett was killed, but the effect that such a horrific occurrence had on Money and Sunnyside left everyone, young and old, devastated and fearing for the safety of themselves and their children.

Racism was widespread throughout the Mississippi Delta. It was so bad that black men were afraid to even look at white women. Many would drop their heads and look another way or even go the opposite direction when approaching a white woman. The killing of Emmett Till was yet another occurrence that put black people on notice of how far Mississippi had yet to come in mending race relations after slavery.

* * *

Emmett wasn't the only black man that was brutalized by white men for a lie that a white woman told. White women telling their husbands that a black man so much as smiled at them could prove deadly, as it often did. White men couldn't wait for night to come to hunt down the black men that allegedly disrespected their women.

The treatment that black men experienced in dealing with white people left them fearful of confronting any of their wrongdoings, including Mr. Bill's. There were some men who would stand up to Mr. Bill's bullying, but when night came, they had to get out of dodge in a hurry. Their lives were on the line, and it would've been no surprise if we had found the same man that stood up to Mr. Bill beaten and left to die the very next day.

White folks believed in beating blacks. I remember one time, Daddy helped Bubba, a young Black man accused of trying to strike a white man, flee Sunnyside one night. Daddy had him hide out under the riverbank until it was time for the Greyhound bus to come through Sunnyside. Around 9:45p.m., he came up from under the dark riverbank and Daddy took him to the highway to catch the bus to get out of Mississippi.

* * *

One afternoon we looked up and saw Mr. Bill driving toward our house in his truck. When he got in the front yard and got out, he had the biggest grin on his face as he approached our porch.

"Will!" he called out to Daddy, propping his foot onto the bottom step of our porch.

Daddy came out of the house and stood in the doorway, confused at what brought Mr. Bill to our house.

"You know my daughters are getting of age," Mr. Bill continued, still smiling with a devilish grin.

"Yessir," Daddy responded, now standing at the edge of the porch.

"Well, you know, Willie, pretty soon you gon' need to start addressin' them as "Miss."

Mr. Bill's oldest daughter was turning sixteen. Denise was our oldest sister, the same age as Mr. Bill's daughter. Mr. Bill would have never thought to address Denise as "Miss."

I stood in awe of Mr. Bill's nerve as he waited for my daddy to respond. I never could digest the fact that we had to say "Miss" to white girls the same age as our sisters.

"Yessir," Daddy said. I could see the anger on his face as he clenched his jaw as to keep any other words from falling out of his mouth.

Mr. Bill's mouth curved upward a little more. He nodded and started back toward his truck. He had a proud look on his face as he climbed into the small brown pickup, blowing the horn and driving away.

Even today, it seems that I can still hear Daddy saying, "Yessir." It just ate me up inside. I couldn't understand what was so important about calling Mr. Bill's daughters "Miss?"Me and my siblings never had to say anything because we made sure we stayed our distance from Mr. Bill's daughter, but my parents work on the plantation always put them in a position to cross path with Mr. Bill's daughter in one way or another.

But on the rare occasion that we did come face-to-face with his daughters, we never called them Miss. They always came with a fake grin, looking just like their daddy and expecting to hear us call them, "Miss."It never happened. We were determined to never address them in that manner.

* * *

Mrs. Betty, Mr. Bill's wife, treated the women on the plantation with more respect. Some of the landowners' wives were kind, but some wouldn't even wave if they saw a black woman walking down the road. Some of them would even speed up to make sure they covered her with the dust from their cars.

Working with a white woman who actually treated black women with kindness made me realize the difference between a white woman who hated black women. Some white women always wore the meanest frown on their faces, looking down on the "poor black women." They carried around with them an air of superiority over them.

Like Mrs. Betty, Mrs. Thomas, another landowner's wife, treated the black women totally different than the mean wives. Women like Mrs. Thomas and Mrs. Betty seemed to be happy to have black women helping them out in their homes.

Many times, the women worked in the homes of the landowners cooking and cleaning. Black women sometimes cared for white women's children when needed.

Despite how we were treated, we were taught to love and respect everyone, regardless of race or color.

"The color of a person's skin don't make 'em, but what's in the heart do," I remember Momma would say.

However, experiencing the scorn of white women, I didn't understand why we had to show so much respect to them.

"Why do we always do what Mrs. Betty required us to do?" I wanted to know what was so special about white people. I was young when I realized that, in the south, black people's lives revolved around white comfortability, especially when it came to white women. If a white woman had to make a pit stop at the corner store and blacks were standing on the porch of the store, they had to move all the way back to the perimeter of the store's porch.

"Will it hurt you to say, "Yes, Ma'am?" Will it take the skin off your back to help unload groceries from a car?" Momma said to me one time, looking me dead in my eyes, her mouth twisted upwards.

I had finally mustered up the courage to ask Momma questions that laid heavy in my spirit for a while, "Why did we have to respect people who didn't respect, or even like us?"

"What would it do to you to just shut your mouth sometimes?" she said, fed up with my rebellion.

I looked at her, wanting to really tell her exactly what it did to me, but I held my tongue and didn't utter another word.

* * *

I was about eleven years old, much too young to voice my opinion; although, I knew what I was hearing and seeing wasn't right: landowners' cursing their workers, physically push them around, their wives speaking down on black women. It was heartbreaking at times not being able to speak up or share my point of view concerning a matter, but I learned to deal with it, and eventually, I found the courage to ask, "Why?" and actually get answers.

The struggles of families around us, the desperation of the workers because of their working conditions and their boss's treatment disturbed me. There were many times I wanted to do something to help but, being a child; there wasn't anything I could do.

As a child, I simply thought that black people didn't take up for themselves because they were afraid of landowners. However, as I matured, I began to understand that fear wasn't their only motivation. Protecting themselves and their loved ones were equally important. Parents knew what needed to be done to ensure that the family was safe.

Our parents knew the most important thing for the family was to be able to stay together under one roof. Our home was a safe space.

There were times I wanted to believe that my parents weren't at all afraid of Mr. Bill. I want to believe they humbled themselves in order to get respect and to keep from having to retaliate when Mr. Bill went on one of his rampages against his workers. They were very careful not to create any problems that could cause Mr. Bill to use unpleasant words at them or consider making them move off the plantation.

* * *

Throughout my childhood, I, along with my brothers and sisters, was sent to church. Sometimes our parents took us. I loved church and didn't mind working on different ministries to help out. Momma got us up almost every Sunday morning for Sunday school. She's laid out our Sunday clothes and cook us a nice breakfast, then send us on our way.

Zion Watt Baptist Church was a small, white country church with a fair number of members. It wasn't fancy or lavishly adorned, but it was a church, and it served its purpose. We could see outside without peeping from the windows, and the pews were made of wood without cushion, but no one ever complained about anything concerning the comfort of the church.

I wish they had because those hard wood pews and chairs would put a hurting on your behind after awhile.

We had service once a month on the first Sunday, but Sunday school was taught every Sunday morning. Our pastor, Pastor Jones, was a brown-skinned, medium build man with a big, round head. He enjoyed eating and loved to talk. When he preached, he always found a way to weave a couple of songs into his sermon. All of the members of Zion Watt loved him.

Going to church really made a difference in my life. It taught me how to love more and how to forgive. When I finally started to experience God, all the anger that I had toward white people began to slowly fade. Memories of hearing and seeing physical and verbal abuse upon others by the landowners faded. For some reason, they didn't burn as brightly in my memories anymore. They weren't all forgotten, but I could look beyond them.

* * *

I can remember incidents happening to certain families during the night that no one knew about until the next day. We would hear of someone's spouse or teenage child missing or found beaten and left to die. There were times we would hear of someone getting shot, stabbed or beaten but the authorities are doing nothing about it. There were many terrible occurrences taking place that were unexplainable and soon forgotten.

Many times, during the heart of winter, families would be forced to move without notice, sometimes for the simple reason of owing the boss money or because someone in the family was caught stealing from the boss.

Etta was my best friend. She lived up the road from me, so every day, she'd come to my house to play. One summer day, Etta didn't come to play. I waited for her, but when I realized that Etta wasn't coming, I asked Momma if I could walk up to her house.

She looked at me with a sense of sadness and without any explanation, all she said was, "No. You can't go up there."

Momma already knew that Etta's family had been forced to move to another plantation. Sometimes families didn't move too far away, and we were still able to see them. But sometimes, families moved, never to be seen again. Our life wasn't all roses, but I must say that we had it much better than some families. I don't ever remember our family being told to move or threatened by Mr. Bill.

I would often go meet Daddy when he was walking home from work.

"Gal, you see how hard me and ya momma work?" Daddy asked me one afternoon, walking him home from work.

"Yessir," I said, listening intently as we walked back and forth between the grass and the roadway to make room for passing cars.

"Working hard is the only thing that's going to help us along the way," he said, patting me on my shoulder, "You can't depend on no one for nothing. You gon' have to find a way or make one," he continued.

When Momma and Daddy talked, I listened to every word that fell from their tongue, whether I liked it or not.

Every few years a different landowner would take over the plantation as the new owner. Mr. Bill sold the plantation to Mr. Jones. Mr. Jones was identical to Mr. Bill mean as a rattle snake. If he had a problem with a worker or didn't like him, for any reason, his disdain didn't go unnoticed.

Mr. Jones had a bad habit of cursing, even when he wasn't angry. He would accuse you of not doing the work you were told to do, always wanting parents to make sure their children were working and not playing around in the field. On top of everything else, he never wanted anyone to take a pee or water break.

The landowners in Sunnyside had this way of instilling fear into their workers and demanding respect even when they were wrong. Though they gave off the sense that they were superior and powerful, I always had a feeling that they were just as afraid of black people as black people were afraid of them.

CHAPTER 3

WHAT WAS IN SYNNYSIDE?

Sunnyside, didn't have a lot of recreational places where people could go for entertainment, especially young kids. We had to create our own fun and games. After years of playing games in which the only things needed was a couple of sticks, an old can, and other kids, we had gotten pretty good at making our own enterta-inment.

Though Sunnyside didn't have the big-time clubs and pool halls that other towns had, it was pretty popular. When my siblings and I talked about Sunnyside to our friends at school, they became intere-sted in coming for a visit. They wanted to see what all of the talks were about and how we had so much fun in such a small and rural area.

To not have much of anything, Sunnyside was filled with things to do. When friends from school would come to visit, we'd go from house to house, hanging out on the porch, playing card games in the yard, anything you could think of. For miles, you could see groups of young guys playing basketball or softball and young ladies playing jack rock or jumping rope. It was so many young people that lived in Sunnyside that there was never a dull moment.

If the games and fellowshipping weren't enough to draw young people from miles around, the young women in Sunnyside would seal the deal. The rumor was Sunnyside had some of the prettiest girls in all of Mississippi. Young guys from surrounding areas would walk for miles just to come to be in the presence of the Sunnyside girls.

On the weekends, Greenwood was the place to be since it was the largest and closest town to Sunnyside. People from all over came to Greenwood to shop and take care of their business. Many people came to Greenwood just to hang out, party, and have a good time. Some people simply enjoyed walking around in town looking in the different stores. Greenwood had stores and shops, cafés, and restaurants, everything you could think of. The cafes played the best music and the bars served the coldest beer and fried the tastiest fish and chicken you'd ever eat.

Sunnyside was barely on the map. It was an unincorporated community that was covered mostly by a cotton and bean plantation. Apart from the plantations, Sunnyside had an elementary school, a Baptist church, a small family-owned grocery store, a gas station, and a utility house for the phone company. Lined along the Sunnyside roads were small houses with huge families living in them.

Our little community didn't have streetlights or sidewalks, but it had a long road that ran from Highway 49 all the way to Money, Mississippi. The main road split off into unpaved side roads where more houses and families lived. As you begin to travel down the Sunnyside Road, the first thing you would see on the right was a huge red brick building–Sunnyside Elementary School. Sunnyside Elementary was where all of the white children from miles around went to learn. In the entire school was not a single black child. Whenever we walked past Sunnyside Elementary during school hours, we knew better than to look too long in the direction of the school, especially if the students were out for recess.

"What you black niggers looking at?" some of them would call to us from the playground if they noticed us watching them as we made our way home.

They'd shake their fists and lick their tongues at us, but they would never come near the road. They'd just watch and taunt us from their shiny monkey bars as we passed by.

"You best stay on that side of the road, Niggers," a tall white boy said to us as me and my siblings walked home one afternoon.

My heart began racing and my palms began to sweat so much that it felt as though my hands were melting. I wondered what we had done so awfully wrong to make him say something so mean to us.

We looked at him for a slight moment, but we didn't say anything. I know that deep down inside, we all wanted to defend ourselves if nothing more than licking our tongues or shaking our fists at him. But we did nothing. We simply kept walking.

Momma would always say, "'Nigger' don't have no color, so you don't need to worry 'bout what somebody else calls you. We Negroes, not niggers."

Regardless of how the kids treated us, I still wanted nothing more than to attend Sunnyside Elementary. It was one of the largest and most beautiful schools in our area. The building was tall and constructed of pretty red bricks line with clean glass windows and large gray doors. The yard was always well-kept and along the lawn were flowers of all colors. A large basketball court sat off to the side of the school building, and just behind the building was a softball field.

When holidays came around, they celebrated inside and outside with beautiful decorations. At Christmastime, a large pine tree with lights that seemed to illuminate the entire street was erected just in front of the school, right across the driveway.

From the outside looking in, it seemed that Sunnyside Elementary had everything it needed and wanted. The only problem was that black children weren't allowed to attend.

Past Sunnyside Elementary were brick homes where the white families lived in Sunnyside. Officer Thomas and his family lived in the first brick home. When I was about fourteen, I worked cleaning Officer Thomas' home on Saturday's to make me a little spending money.

Past the nice brick homes was our neck of the woods– the real Sunnyside community. In the area where black people lived, there weren't any decent homes anywhere along the Sunnyside road for miles. The only nice homes on our side of the road were the Slawson's and their daughter's, who owned the grocery store and gas station.

The main road that split Sunnyside right down the middle was the only paved road in the area for many years. The moment we turned off the pavement, it became gravel, from gravel to dirt and mud, which led right to the Gin Lott.

Pass all the small homes and the grocery store was an intersection with a large white house that belonged to one of the landowners. The large house sat on many acres of land as far as the eye could see. Across the lawn were trees and flowers of all kind that bore pecans, walnuts, pears, and plums. Our parent's dared us to touch or go near any of those trees because the landowners threaten to shoot anyone they caught picking from them.

* * *

Reality set in the moment we turned off the black, paved road. We knew we were close to home because we had to walk through tall grass and dirt paths that became muddy when it rained. Small posits of wet dirt would seep through our hole-ridden shoes as we trekked along the trails to reach home.

At the bend of the curve down one of the dirt roads was Zion Watt Missionary Baptist Church, a small, white building with wooden steps leading up to the front entrance and clear windows made of what appeared to be "fiber glass." Everyone in the Sunnyside community attended Zion Watt. Once a month for many years, everyone came to church to lay their burdens down.

Though the church was barely able to fit all of its members, the location of the new Zion Watt on Sunnyside Road was better than what we'd previously experienced. Zion Watt was in a new location, but the building was all but new. The furniture was old and rickety, and the wooden pews didn't have cushions. We didn't even have a box fan, leaving us to fan ourselves with handheld paper fans, letting up the windows to get a breeze when one decided to come by. For the colder months, Zion Watt had two gas heaters. One sat in the back of the church in the corner, and one sat at the front near the side entrance across from the pulpit.

* * *

The carpetless floor made for a wonderful percussion when the saints would become so overjoyed by the music that they'd stamp their feet in unison in synchrony with the drummer. Even though we never had an air conditioner in the summertime to cool us off or cushion pews to sit on, we loved our church and always looked forward to going when our Sunday was approaching.

After leaving the old location, Zion Watt became one of the finest churches in the community, and no one complained about no longer having to walk down dirt roads to get to church on Sunday.

Although the old Zion Watt Church building was abandoned for many years, the land around the church continued to be used as the community cemetery. Anyone who died was buried on the old Zion Watt Church ground.

Whenever someone died in Sunnyside, the men would go to the barn where all the mules and horses were kept, climb up to the top, and ring the large bell. The bell would sound all over Sunnyside for miles. People from near and far could hear the toning of the bell. Eventually, people would begin to gather, asking questions to find out who had died. The men would ring the bell over and over again to make sure everyone knew that someone had passed. Whenever someone died, a cloud of sorrow hung over the whole community that day.

Sometimes it would take the hearse all day to come to pick up the body. Because of the location of our house, the hearse had to pass us going and coming back. The sight of that hearse coming to take the poor old body no longer living always made me uneasy. When the hearse would pass, it appeared to be moving in slow motion. I remember running and hiding many times, trying to cover up my face whenever I saw the hearse coming. Every few days, it seemed as though the hearse was making its way past our house.

If visions of that hearse in my head didn't scare me enough, the darkness of nighttime sure did. Living in the country, when night would come, the darkness engulfed everything under the sky. It would get so dark that you couldn't see your hand in front of your face. With the trees towering over our houses, the moon's light didn't have a chance of reaching our little old shack on the river bank.

Most churches had service once a month because most pastors had three or four churches in different areas. One church wasn't enough to pay the bills. Most of the churchgoers didn't have transportation to get to church, so they had to just wait for service to be hosted at a location that was within walking distance from them. The churchgoers who did have a car never bothered to go to another church when their church didn't have service either. When we didn't have Sunday service, we still attended Sunday school almost every Sunday morning. After all, besides the Pastor, we had only one other deacon that was able to read and teach the Bible.

Once a month, our pastor came to Zion Watt on Sunnyside Road for service. Every month, the saints would gather together their earnings to pay "dues" to the church. Even though the church building would be packed to capacity, sometimes the dues collected would be no more than a hand full of dollar bills, less than twenty dollars at times.

During the three Sundays when there weren't any services, people lived like heathens: fighting, drinking, and stealing from each other. Once their meeting Sunday rolled around, everyone was ready to take their burdens to the altar, but no one was willing to take their dollars. Despite not being able to have service every Sunday, whenever the saints did come together, we would have a Holy Ghost good time at Zion Watt. The spirits were always high, and the music had the power to stir your very soul.

We had about eight choir members, and our musician, Sister Strong, was our school bus driver. She played every song in the same key.

Once during the month, Sister Strong would organize a choir practice to prepare for Sunday service, and believe me, we sounded just like we practiced, singing the same songs every Sunday. One of Sister Strong's favorite songs was "He's Sweet I Know." We got so tired of that song, but our obedience outweighed our annoyance, so if she played it, we sang it.

One Easter Sunday morning, when it was time for us to sing, our musician couldn't seem to get the piano to play. The piano had never once been tuned, and it sounded like it had a bad cold, creaking and wheezing throughout every performance. We all stood in the choir stand, dressed in our Easter Sunday's best, waiting for that nod from Sister Strong to begin singing.

As we rose up, you could hear the sound of those wooden chairs scrubbing the wooden floor. The noise echoed all over the church, but Mrs. Strong dared us to even smile. Eventually, the piano began to work, and Mrs. Strong nodded to us.

"He's sweet I know. He's sweet I know. Dark clouds may rise, and strong winds may blow," we all sang in unison as the saints began to rise from their seats to join the organized worshippers, "But I can tell the world, wherever I may go that I found a Savior and he's sweet I know."

The music and message always kept the energy flowing throughout the service, but the characters of the church always had a way of keeping me entertained.

One night during revival, Mr. West, one of the deacons, fell backwards in his chair, giving us all a show. Mr. West liked sitting at the back of the church during revival time to control the younger children and keep them quiet during the service. He didn't want us to move a muscle during service, watching us like a hawk. If any of us did so much as sneezed, up to the Mourner's Bench, we'd go. Since our parents weren't there with us, Mr. West took it upon himself to make sure the children stayed in line. Most of the time, parents would drop their children off at church for service, then pick them up after service let out. But somehow, parents still knew exactly what was going on at church where their children were concerned. They knew if their children were on the Mourner's Bench before the revival was even over.

On this the particular night, the deacon had really gotten into the service. Somehow, he forgot that he was reared back against the wall on the two hind legs of his wooden chair. Mr. West was always one of the saints that enjoyed howling and edging the preacher on.

"Go 'head preach," he began to howl, waving his hand in the air as if he were fanning away the heat that built up inside the packed church.

All of a sudden, that chair slipped from under him, and his body was thrown to the floor like a sack of potatoes. The noise was so loud you could've sworn that the back of the church had collapsed and fallen to the ground. Startled, everyone looked around frantically, searching for the source of the commotion.

Mr. West scrambled to get up from the floor, seemingly hopeful no one noticed his blunder, but he didn't get up fast enough.

As young children, we couldn't contain our amusement, and we laughed him to scorn. The more he tried to quiet us, the more we laughed.

During a revival, the Pastor expected anyone who hadn't accepted the Lord as their personal savior to come and dedicate their life. Every night for a whole week, the preacher would deliver a powerful message and wait for the spirit to move. Parents would force their children up to the Mourner's Bench; the front pew was where everyone who hadn't been saved yet sat.

Amazingly, the bench was always filled with children. I don't ever remember an adult coming up to repent or be saved. It was always the children that needed to be saved. Luckily for us, our parents never forced us to go sit on the mourner's bench.

During one of the revivals, I went to the Mourner's Bench on my own.

"When you feel the spirit moving, yagotta go," I remember Momma would tell us.

So, I waited, expecting to feel something.

Usually, I and my brothers and sisters would just sit back and watch other children walk up to the front pew. They always had a scared look on their faces, and they moved slowly, dragging their feet as if they had cement in their shoes.

Many of them would sit on that bench night after night, and I'm sure they were in the same predicament as me–waiting to feel something but never knowing what exactly we were waiting to feel. On the last day of the revival, I walked to the row of children who were, once again, waiting anxiously to "feel something." The pastor approached the podium on the altar that seemed to rise high above the congregation.

"Praise the Lord, Saints; he greeted the packed church.

"Praise the Lord," they responded in unison.

As Pastor continued the sermon, none of the children moved from their seats.

"Now, those of you who don't come up here and accept the Lord tonight, y'allgon' miss out!" he shouted, hoping that fear would be a great enough feeling to get us moving toward the mourner's bench.

I sat up in my seat.

"Miss out on what?" the question lingered in my head, "Getting saved? Going to heaven?"

I'd heard of heaven and hell, but I didn't know too much about them. All I knew was that whatever they were, they were real and no one wanted to take that chance of missing heaven and going to hell.

I decided that I would wait a little while longer to see if I was going to feel the Holy Spirit. Sometimes, I would look around the church just to make sure that if the Holy Spirit did slide in the middle of one of Pastor's sermons, I didn't miss out on seeing it.

The preacher knew that he only had one night left before the revival was over, and it seemed as though he couldn't stand the thought of not having one person come forward to dedicate their lives to the Lord. So, just before he closed out, he began looking around the church to see if any of the children even attempted to part with their seats and come forward, submitting ourselves to the Mourner's Bench. Still fearing that he wasn't going to get not one soul to accept the Lord, he pulled his last trick out of his sleeve.

"Now, for any one of you that want to give your life to God, I got a shiny nickel for you if you come right now," he said, breathing heavily into the microphone and digging into the pocket of his pants.

When we heard that he was giving a whole nickel for anyone who came forward, it seemed like every child in the church suddenly wanted to be saved. That night, I went up to the mourner's Bench with all of the other children. On top of needing that nickel, I refused to be the only one left in the pew.

As we waited for the pastor to find enough nickels to give to each child, I had already begun making plans for exactly how I was going to spend that nickel. A nickel went a long way back in the day, and that was an opportunity that I couldn't miss out on.

We were all paid to come up and sit on the Mourner's Bench that night, but I doubt that any of us had a clue of what sitting on the Mourner's Bench even meant.

I still didn't know what the Holy Spirit felt like, but I surely knew how a nickel felt.

When Sunday morning finally came around, we were all ready to go down to the water to be baptized.

"They went down in the water a dry devil and came up a wet devil," the old folks would say of those who got baptized with no true intention of changing their lives.

None of us felt anything in our hearts, but the feeling of that nickel in our pockets was just enough to appease our longing for the time being.

We were young and didn't have the slightest idea of what we were really doing getting baptized. Accepting the Lord as your personal savior was never explained to us in a way that we could understand.

We all were just playing church and doing whatever the next kid was doing.

Momma wasn't too happy about us selling our souls to the Lord for a nickel.

"Now, y'all know you should'a asked me before y'all found your up to that altar pretending to get saved," she told us, laying out our all-white in preparation for our baptisms.

Even though momma didn't always go to church with us, she wasn't the one to take God lightly. I remember her whipping us one time for what she called "playing with the Lord," when she found us on the front porch hooping and hollering like the grown folks did in church.

Everyone that lived in the Sunnyside community got baptized in the Tallahatchie River. The river was right across the road from the church, so following service, all of the churchgoers would walk down the hill to the banks of the river to watch those who gave their lives to Christ be baptized. Dressed in our white baptism robes with plastic bags covering our heads, we walked slowly to the water, singing hymns and praying. Even though baptisms were a serious occasion, on the Sunday that all the children decided to be baptized, we couldn't help but be amused at the sight of each of our friends being dunked into the water and come up flailing like fish. We stood on the bank of the river, holding in our chuckles as each of us, one by one, waded into the water where Pastor was standing.

"In obedience to our Lord and savior, and upon confession of your faith in him, I baptize you in the name of the Father, Son, and the Holy Ghost," the Pastor would say while dipping each of us into the water.

After the baptisms, we all went back to the church to eat and celebrate the newly received servants of God. Next to our church was a large building used as the fellowship hall. On special Sundays such as Church Anniversary, or Homecoming the women would get together and cook up all sorts of delicious food. Everyone would come together and bring something to share. The feast would last for hours.

Sometimes people would bring so much food that we'd run out of space in the fellowship hall, so they'd end up serving the churchgoers from the trunks of their cars. There was fried chicken, rice, green beans, fresh bread, homemade lemonade, iced tea, and every kind of cake or pie you could think of.

We would have a good old-fashioned time, and there was always plenty of food to take home.

* * *

Many years later, after the church stopped having large gatherings, the fellowship hall was converted into a recreation center. At first, the center was used to have bingo nights for the elders, but about a year or so later, the "Zion Watt Fellowship Hall" was renamed the "Club House," which changed its entire use. People began using it for what they called "clubbing," Saturday night dancing and drinking and getting merry like Christmas.

When we got older, my parents started letting us go hang out at the club house occasionally. At least once a month, they would have some type of activity, mostly birthday parties or dance socials. We would dance from the time we got there until time to go home.

One year, Walter decided that he would talk the owner into letting him have a birthday celebration for a friend of his. There were many people at the party and everyone seemed to be having a good time. Next thing they knew, beer bottles were flying across the room. A fight had broken out and because of the crowdedness in the small building it spiraled out of control before anyone could see where the commotion was coming from. Needless to say, Momma never let us step foot in the club house again for a long time.

Next to the club house was a phone utility building where the phone company workers would come and check the wiring and troubleshoot problems with the phone services in the community. I don't remember any blacks having a telephone in Sunnyside except for the store owners.

Most blacks couldn't afford a telephone. We thought that owning a phone was only for white people or blacks that had money. We mostly communicated through letters and post cards. The Slawsons had a phone in their store. They'd let people come to the store to use it if they needed to make a call, usually for an emergency. Mrs. Slawson would allow Momma to give family mem-bers that lived out of town the store's number, and she'd come by and give Momma messages they'd leave.

The neighborhood corner store was located right next to the utility house. Everyone loved that little store. People from miles around would come to that store to do a little shopping or get some gas. Mr. and Mrs. Slawson owned and operated the corner store.

The corner store had everything people needed, and the atmosphere was welcoming and animated. There were seats on the porch and inside the store for people to sit around and chat. On the weekends, all the plantation workers, especially the men, would come together at the store and fellowship. They would hang out and vent together. Sometimes there would be so many people at that store; it was hard to find a parking spot. The gatherers would park wherever they could, lining their cars up along the road on both sides.

They'd sit around smoking, drinking beer, and talking for hours. The store was the perfect place for the workers to come together after a long and stressful week of working hard on the plantation. It was also the perfect place to hear the stories they would tell, everyone with a better story than whoever was telling theirs at the moment, making it hard for anyone to get a word in.

When Daddy would come home after being at the store with his buddies, he always wanted to share what they talked about with Momma.

"Gon' somewhere with that lie and foolishness, Will," Momma would interject, but Daddy would insist on trying to convince her that everything he was saying was something worth hearing and was indeed true.

"Swea' 'fore God," Daddy would say, raising his right hand to God. My favorite stories were the ones about Mr. Wallace.

Mr. Wallace was Daddy's friend. He'd hang at the store with the rest of the men, and Daddy would always sucker Mr. Wallace into giving them a show. Mr. Wallace was a tall, skinny, dark-skinned man. Despite his speech impediment because of his lack of teeth to hold together his words, he wanted to be a pastor and swore up and down that he could preach.

Daddy was good about making a fool of people. He would boost this poor man up to give the folks at the store a sermon. Then, Daddy would come home and try to reenact the sermon for Momma, just how Mr. Wallace performed it. Daddy could imitate anybody.

Daddy's shenanigans almost never amused Momma, but we would laugh hysterically at Daddy fumbling over Bible verses and waving his hands to heaven like a maniac, then he would start jumping around as if he had the Holy Ghost.

All of the other men that hung around at the Slawson's store were just like Daddy–high-spirited, storytellers just looking for a good time. That's the kind of men who would carry on for hours at that store.

Sometimes the front of the store would be so crowded that it would be hard to even get inside. Most times, you had to physically work your way through the crowd of sweaty, beer breath and tractor oil-smelling men just to pick up a loaf of bread or pay for a gallon of gas.

For many years, the Slawsons owned the only store and gas station in Sunnyside. In addition to their southern hospitality and community telephone, they had the best snacks in the world. On the counter was a long line of glass jugs filled with every snack a kid could dream of–pickles, bubble gum, candy, and coconut cookies for a penny apiece. We only ever had enough money to buy a cookie **or** a penny candy, but we didn't mind; the cookies were the best thing in the store. Fifteen cents could get you a whole sack full of cookies, and if by chance you came up to a quarter, the possibilities were endless in the Slawson's store.

Ms. Sarah, the Slawson's daughter, owned a big house right beside the store. If nothing else about the Slawson's showed their wealth, their house was proof that the Slawsons were loaded and probably didn't want for anything.

Passing Ms. Sarah's house, the small homes lining the right side of the road became old shacks again. On the left side of the road was the Tallahatchie River. Our house sat on the river's bank, facing fields of cotton, beans, corn, and sorghum crops. We lived so close to the Tallahatchie River that we could fish from our back door. When it rained for a long period of time, the river would rise up high and the water would come up to our back door. Sometimes the water would flow into the house.

Daddy used to have an old boat that he loved to go fishing in every chance he got, taking Roger or Walter with him. Since we lived so close to the river, Daddy never took his boat out of the water. He just left it tied to a tree stump year-round.

At the end of the road was a deep curve that led to the Gin Lott, where our house was. It was called the Gin Lott because there was a working cotton gin that was located just past our house. The Gin Lott was always covered by the scent of gas, oil, and different chemicals. The Gin Lott was paved with dirt that got muddy when it rained.

CHAPTER 4

OUR HOME IN THE GIN LOTT

Although our house didn't look like much from the outside, what was on the inside made all the difference. The love shared between members of the Tanner family made the small shack at the edge of the woods warm and cozy. We didn't have much furniture or decorative items, but we had peace and content-ment.

Our house looked much like an old beat up barn. Our two older sisters were born in Silver City, Mississippi but moved to Sunnyside when they were very young. My four younger siblings and I were all born and raised in the Gin Lott.

There were three houses that sat in the Gin Lott–our house, Uncle Wilbert and Henry's, Momma's stepfather. All of the houses were pretty much in the same condition– rotted from the floor to the ceiling. Windows were old with cracked panes and not a lick of paint on them. Every room needed painting and repairs. Whenever it rained, the roof would leak like a waterfall.

We had to set buckets and pans all over the four-room, tin-roofed house. All the doors had large cracks and holes in them. They were usually wide enough to put your fist through.

We had a long front porch with three steps to walk up to the front entrance. The two front rooms had their own separate entrance. Our large front yard gave us enough space to play whatever games we chose, but since we lived so close to the Tallahatchie River, a backyard was nonexistent.

The room on the right side of the house was Daddy and Momma's bedroom with a dual function as the family room where we gathered and entertained ourselves. We would all sit around the fireplace eating and engaging in joyful conversation.

The four youngest slept with Momma and Daddy on one of the two full-sized beds. The mattress on each bed was made of cotton, which was called a tick. The ticks were split down the middle in order to add the cotton and to fluff the mattress when needed. With my younger siblings being small children, wetting the bed happened often enough to require the cotton to be changed periodically. All of our beds were set in old, cast-iron frames that had become rusted. Slats on the bottom supported the mattresses.

On the left side of our house was another front room, which served as a living room and a bedroom. Denise, Anita and I shared that room. We thought it was one of the best rooms in the house. In our room was a full-sized iron bed that slept all three of us, a fireplace, a small bench, and two wooden chairs. There was a homemade closet in the right corner of the room made of boards with nails for hanging our best clothes to keep them out of the dust. It also had a curtain that Momma made to hang across the front, which added a fancy look.

Momma taught all of us how to make up beds by stirring up the cotton and fluffing it to make it look full. However, after every night's sleep, by the morning, those ticks would be flat as a pancake. So, every morning the ticks had to be fluffed and patted evenly. We didn't have a clue of what a real mattress felt like until many years later.

There were two windows and a fireplace with a mantle over it where our radio sat along with Daddy's Prince Albert chewing tobacco. A few pictures hung over the mantle with nails holding them to the wall.

There was also a nail to hang the car keys and a mason jar that sat on the mantle to store pins, needles, and buttons. On the side of the fireplace was a pile of wood and a fire iron for stirring the fire. In front of the fireplace was a long, homemade wooden bench.

In the family room, there was an old chest with drawers where Momma kept clothes. There was also a tall cabinet that was used for storing Daddy's guns. Daddy owned a lot of guns of all types that he used to hunt.

Every door in our house barely hung in place. In order to keep the doors shut, we had a large nail that was bent to wrap around the door to close it as much as it could be closed. Even though the door was left unlocked at times, we didn't worry about being robbed or someone trying to break into our home. Everyone knew that no one had anything worth stealing or breaking into someone else's home for.

All the doors that lead to the outside were secured with what was called a "night latch." Everyone had a night latch on their doors. They were easy to make. All it took was a long, wide piece of wood put across the door that fitted into wooden slots placed on each side of the door.

We didn't have a television, but we did just fine entertaining ourselves with fellowship and the radio. Sometimes we would crack pecans or have popcorn for snacks. We had a large, black, cast iron pot with a top that Daddy would sit on the fire and pop corn. We enjoyed sitting around the fire, eating and telling jokes at night. Daddy and mama had great senses of humor. After a long day, they knew how to bring the family together for a fun-filled night.

We stored everything that we didn't use regularly in the "junk room." The junk room was off limits, especially at night because of the rats that made their dwelling amid all of the junk. There were so many huge rats that lived inside the junk room that we were terrified to even go near it. Whatever we needed from that room, we made sure to get it before nightfall.

Though most of the rats stayed in the junk room throughout the night, some would manage to find their way into the living parts of the house. The rats that we had were too smart to be caught in some makeshift trap. To catch these rats, you would need a shotgun or some gasoline and matches.

Sometimes we would lie in bed at night and watch them run back and forth in the loft. Momma kept her cornmeal, flour, lard, and sugar in large containers with tight lids to keep the rats from getting into them. The rats would destroy any and everything in their path, so we had to hide everything from them. They would cut and chew up our clothes and shoes every chance they got.

Our entire house had wooden plank floors with cracks throughout. If you moved the wrong way, you were bound to get a splinter in your foot. There were wide cracks in the plank floors, and like the rats, the cold wind would find its way through the cracks. We could look through the floors and see the chickens, dogs or cats running underneath the house.

Daddy would spray a pesticide called DDT to keep the insects and other creatures away, but DDT had no effect on the rats. Daddy would spray the pesticide outside the house for snakes and up in the loft for the mice.

Mr. Bill used the same pesticide for his field to keep insects from eating away at his crops. We would be working out in the fields and Mr. Bill would have the airplanes fly over the field, spraying the cotton with DDT. He didn't think twice about the people working in the field. The DDT would cause us to break out into coughing fits. Our eyes would burn and our nose would run for what seemed like hours. Momma would tell us to cover our faces when the planes flew over. Our straw hats and long sleeve shirts would shield some of the poison, but never enough.

* * *

Our house had so many rifts during the winter and daddy would try to insulate our windows and doors. He would cut pieces of durable plastic to fit over each opening of the house. Then he would nail planks of wood over cracks and holes in the floor and walls. Daddy did this every year in order, trying to keep our house warm during the winter.

The kitchen had two entrances: through the door from our parents' room and the door from me and my sisters' room. I hated going into the kitchen for anything in the winter because no heat flowed into it. The temperature would drop so low in our house during the winter months that the buckets of water that were used for cooking or running baths would freeze solid. Momma would sit the bucket of water on the fireplace to unthaw it. Our drinking water was kept by the fireplace during the night just in case we needed water in the middle of the night.

When our kitchen stove broke down, Momma cooked every meal on the fireplace. She knew how to place the logs on the fire to balance her pots on top of them. She'd make greens, beans, and peas. She even made cornbread on the fireplace using a cast iron skillet. Momma could flip a hoe cake of flour bread like a professional, never letting it fall or tear. Eventually, we were blessed to get another wood burning iron stove with tin pipes that extended out of the wall. Momma no longer had to bend over at that hot fireplace to prepare our meals.

For the longest, I despised going into that cold, dim kitchen in the winter, but once Momma got that wooden iron stove, the atmosphere was different. When Momma would cook, the air would fill with an aroma that was out of this world. My favorite meal was when Momma would make homemade biscuits and onion gravy with fat back or cured ham. Most of the time there was no meat, just onion gravy and biscuits or homemade sugar syrup and a bread hoecake. Hoe cakes were just flat pieces of bread cooked in a cast iron skillet on top of the stove.

We didn't have running water just pump water that we got from the tractor shed every day. The pump had to be primed or it would freeze up in the winter. Daddy would have to put heat to the pump to unfreeze it so that we could get water. The water was hard to use as drinking water because of its terrible taste, so we mostly used it for cooking, bathing, and washing. We had to get our drinking water from a well down the road from our house. The water from the well was so smooth and refreshing. Everyone came to the well to get their drinking water.

We would carry the water in large jugs and buckets from the well all the way home. I would get tired of carrying those heavy jugs and buckets of water every day, so sometimes, I would only fill my container up partially and let my brothers and sisters do the real heavy lifting with their jugs filled to the brim. Whenever I refused to fill my bucket to the top, they'd tell our parents. It never made sense to fill each jug or bucket up to the brim if we would have to come to get more the next day anyway, so I was only concerned with getting enough water to make it through the night.

Of all of the places in our home, we always found our way to the front porch to enjoy each other's company, even if flies and mosquitoes swarmed us every time; we stepped foot out the door. We had some enjoyable moments on the porch. One night after dinner, as we all sat outside, a giant frog leaped onto the porch. My siblings and I hopped up and ran into the house squealing, but Momma and Daddy didn't move. They watched us in laughter as we clamored to get into the house. After a minute, the frog leaped back onto the ground and disappeared into the darkness.

CHAPTER 5

THE GIN LOTT

The Gin Lott was the heart of Sunnyside. Most of the plantation's farm equipment and supplies were stored in the Gin Lott. The cotton gin on the Gin Lott was in operation for many years, processing the cotton and beans. In the fifties, farm operations greatly changed. People no longer had to walk behind mules and horses and use manual equipment to farm. Instead, machinery had improved methods in agriculture production. Even though technology decreased landowners' reliance on animals, much of the more strenuous labor was still being done by people.

My family worked in the fields chopping and picking cotton. We chopped rows of cotton from one end of the field to the other, making sure to clear weeds and grass along the way and thinning out cotton that was too thick in places.

Our heads were always on a swivel, looking out for snakes that hid under the cotton in efforts to hide themselves from the sun. I was terrified of snakes. I sometimes found myself working harder to watch out for snakes than cut the cotton. Needless to say, I ended up cutting down more cotton than weeds.

Picking cotton was backbreaking work. Sometimes we had to pick on our knees if the cotton was too low to the ground. We'd have to drag those heavy cotton sacks from one end of the field to the other after filling them up. A six-foot sack usually took hours to fill up, especially if you were a slow picker. Once the sack was filled with cotton, we had to empty it into a trailer that sat at the end of the rows of cotton and start all over. Often, I found myself staring at the sun with tears and sweat streaming down my face, desiring so badly to be free from the hard labor of the unforgiving plantation, but I couldn't. I had to continue to work to help our parents. The work we got from the plantation was our only means of survival.

* * *

My parents had five girls and two boys. We were well-known throughout Sunnyside, and Momma and Daddy were loved by all. They could be found at our neighbors' house fellowshipping on any given day. While my parents talked with our neighbors, we were out and about playing with their kids. We went to church and school together, worked together in the fields, farming and gathered together for social events.

Our Uncle Wilber and Aunt Rosetta, his wife, and our step-grandfather Henry also lived on the Gin Lott. Uncle Wilber and Aunt Rosetta lived in the first "shot gun" house beside the workshop. They were an odd couple. Uncle Wilber was always so mean to Aunt Rosetta, forcing her to pack up and leave him one day. Uncle Wilber would accuse Aunt Rosetta of cheating and would beat her just because he knew that he could. Aunt Rosetta would never fight him back; she was a sweet lady with a good heart. She was always willing to help someone, but Uncle Wilber didn't seem to notice. Uncle Wilber and Aunt Rosetta sold snacks and sodas from the front room of their house. Sometimes, Aunt Rosetta would slip us a cookie or two, free of charge.

On the other side of our house was Henry's. We didn't care too much for Henry. To us, he was nothing but a hateful little man without a good bone in his body. He was nothing but an old liar and a thief. He would steal the salt out of bread and lie on anybody. He was always up to no good.

Our house sat in the middle of Uncle Wilber's and Henry's.

In front of our house, slightly to the left, was a large white barn-like building where corn and other grains were stored. Beside the barn was a tractor shed that kept all the farm equipment and sheep.

Mr. Bill had a field full of sheep. Every day, I used to watch the sheep graze, eating the grass and berries along the fence. They would flock close together, looking for a place to graze since the area was so small. Sometimes, they would just stand and stare, almost as if they were hoping to one day be moved to a bigger pasture, where they could graze freely. After a while, it seemed as though Mr. Bill heard their silent prayer because he decided to move them out of the shed and down the road to a larger pasture.

Though I enjoyed watching the sheep, I was glad they were gone. The foul odor from their manure was awful, and the aroma would linger in the air for miles. We would have to go into the tractor shed to pump water for cooking and bathing, and sometimes the smell would be unbearable, almost to the point of making our eyes water. There would be so much manure on the ground that every step we made was with caution. It was like playing hopscotch, trying to avoid stepping in it.

Every time we came inside the fence, the sheep would scatter. Little did they know that we were just as fearful of them as they were of us.

Once a year, during the early spring, the farm workers would shave the sheep. They called it shearing. They had to shave the sheep to keep them cool and comfortable during the summer. By shearing them in the early spring, the sheep had plenty of time to grow a full coat of wool before the winter came again. The workers would cut all the sheep's wool and Mr. Bill would sell it. Back then, wool was useful for making clothes-- mostly knit socks, sweaters and blankets. People also used it to make furniture covers for chairs and upholstery of all sorts.

Near the shed were two huge long white tanks. One was a propane tank that was used for fueling the farm tractors. It held about ten thousand gallons of propane. Right beside it was a five thousand-gallon tank with gasoline for fueling the combiners and cotton pickers. The combiner was used to separate the grains from the chaff. When it was running, it appeared that the combiner would be chewing up stalks of grain and spitting out hulls.

There were several times one of the tanks caught fire because of the negligence of the tractor driver. The workers would sometimes forget about the tanks. They'd throw the butts of old cigarettes onto the ground and cause the end of the gas hose to catch fire. One time, I watched as one of the workers scrambled to shut off the gas valves and get the fire under control. Sometimes, they would really have to battle that flame to put out the fire. Depending on the swiftness of the worker, a small flame would quickly turn into a catastrophe. We lived way out in the country, so to get any kind of emergency help in time would have been nearly impossible. Luckily, the fire never grew so out of control because if it had, it would've destroyed the entire Gin Lott.

* * *

Every morning, the plantation workers would meet Mr. Bill at the shop at the same time. Mr. Bill would give them their instructions regarding where they'd be working for the day.

Henry worked for Mr. Bill too, and Mr. Bill always found a reason to pick on him, knowing Henry would be too afraid to defend himself. Henry was terrified of Mr. Bill. His knees would tremble the moment he saw Mr. Bill walking toward him. He'd whip Henry as if he were his child. Henry never once even tried to defend himself. He often said that he wanted to fight back, but he was afraid that Mr. Bill might shoot him. I remember once when Mr. Bill jumped from his truck on to Henry, kicking and punching him. Mr. Bill would accuse Henry of lying and not doing his job, but his accusations usually had no truth to them.

Every so often, Mr. Bill would be in a playful mood, cracking jokes, trying to get a laugh out of the workers. No one ever really laughed. They just gave a fake grin. It was hard to predict what Mr. Bill's mood would be and when that mood would change. So, the workers kept their guards up, always waiting for hell to break loose.

The workers all had different chores and tasks. Some would plow the fields, getting it ready for planting. Depending on the time of year, some would be cultivating the harvest of cotton, beans, corn, or wheat. The men walked across the levees, making sure every inch of the rice field got watered. Walking the levees was a dangerous job because they had to walk every inch of the field, even areas where poisonous snakes were known to congregate. The levees were built to prevent water from leaving a certain location. The farm workers would use a tractor with a certain kind of blade to cut the trenches to create the levee wall. They would work for days building levee walls all over huge fields for many miles.

The Gin Lott was loud and busy, and the fumes that rose from the equipment created clouds of pollution, but it was still home.

When morning came, we were awakened by the sound of Tractors, Combiners, horns blowing, and trailers rolling over rocks and gravel. Midst the hustle and bustle of the machinery, we could also hear workers laughing and talking.

When all of the farm equipment was oiled and gassed up, the men would leave for the fields, and the noise would cease. There was such a quietness that covered the Gin Lott, and when the workers would leave for hours, there would be complete silence.

Just a short distance from our house was a pasture enclosed by a barbed-wire fence where all of the horses and mules were kept. The cotton gin that was once used for processing the cotton and beans sat in the middle of the pasture.

When the workers would bring cotton or beans to the gin for processing, they had to make sure at all times that the gates to the pasture were closed, so the animals wouldn't escape. Sometimes, when we'd go to the store, we'd take a shortcut through the pasture. The animals there would chase us, forcing us to run back and climb through the barbed wire fence to safety. The barbed wire would leave scrapes and cuts on our skin and rips in our clothes. Sometimes, the animals didn't bother us. They'd just stand there, watching us go by. Just like Mr. Bill, it was hard to predict what mood the animals would be in; so, we just kept watch and hurried along before any of them decided to change their mind in allowing us to walk through their pasture.

When I was alone, I never took the shortcut through the pasture. I always took the long way around. I was afraid to even walk on the same side of the road as the animals. My brothers, on the other hand, didn't have a problem with the animals unless they weren't in a good mood. They knew when to stay their distance to keep from getting hurt. When we walked down the road, we would pick black berries along the fence for Momma to make black berry pies and jam. I always chose to pick the berries on the side of the fence farthest away from the animals.

CHAPTER 6
OUR FAMILY BOND

The Tanner family was poor in wealth but rich in love and even richer in spirit. Our family ties were a foundation of support. Without our strong family relationship, we wouldn't have had the stability to stand during hard times. Having such a strong bond helped to alleviate our family's emotional stress from time to time. The quality time that we spent together developed our genuine enjoyment for one another's company.

We played games like jack rocks, jump rope, softball, basketball, marbles, and hopscotch to pass the time away. With nothing to occupy our time, we became master game-makers, creating games from whatever materials we had on hand. Our favorite game was stick ball. We spent hours batting small rocks with sticks, seeing whose rock would fly the furthest. "Little Sally Walker" and "Mary Mack" were hand games we liked to play.

"Miss Mary Mack, Mack, Mack. All dressed in black, black, black with silver buttons, buttons, buttons. All down her back, back, back," we'd sing, clapping out hands together and patting our thighs with each beat.

Sometimes we'd get old car tires and roll them around the front yard, pretending they were running automobiles. Dust would rise from the ground like a real car. After rolling the tires around all day long, our hands would be drenched in sweat and dust.

During the day, we'd usually play together in our front yard and on our front porch. Momma and Daddy had a problem with us going to other folks' houses. They hardly ever let us bring our friends into the house, but we had a wonderful time playing in the yard. Mostly every Saturday our friends came to our house to play.

I remember how strict Momma was about us playing in the open fields in front of our house. She never wanted us going out of her sight, especially with other children. If our friends wanted water, we had to take them to the pump across the road near the tractor shed.

"It's not a good idea to visit too much," Momma would tell us, "Too many things tend to happen when you away from home."

We usually took momma's advice and stayed home as much as we could, but Walter always found a reason to go over somebody's house. Walter thought everyone was his friend, no matter the age. Whenever Walter would go off and stay longer than he should, Momma would greet him at the front door with four switches twisted together.

We talked about everything with one another–stories of what we'd done at school, who got into a fight on the school bus, and Daddy loved talking about where'd he'd worked for the day and how many acres he plowed. Momma and Daddy made sure to listen to each and every one of our stories. The conversation always seemed to end with us talking about what we wanted to be when we grew up and where we wanted to live when we finally decided to leave Sunnyside. Momma always expressed to us that she didn't want us to go far away.

Sometimes the conversations would be a little less delightful. There were no secrets that the Tanner family didn't share, and there was nothing hidden that didn't come to light. If for any reason any of us misbehaved and an adult had to get on to us, we would tell our parents before anyone got the chance to tell them on our behalf.

Our family was a circle of strength and support built on a foundation of communication and compassion for one another. When one of us was sick, we all took care of the ill, nursing them back to health.

We even shared one another's chores to help carry each other's load. My sisters and I normally did the inside chores—washing the dishes, cleaning the rooms, sweeping and mopping. But we often helped our brothers with their chores. Countless times my sister and I took on the responsibility of cutting the wood and bringing in water for our brothers.

* * *

Momma and Daddy never had much money, so we never got the chance to go to places like the zoo or Disney World. We ate hoe cakes more times than I would have liked, and our shoes were made of cardboard bottoms.

We *knew* what it felt like to go without—without having the right clothes to go to school, without having the transportation to go to the doctor, without new clothes that hadn't been worn and passed down.

We were all too familiar with going without. We may have been poor in money, but we were rich in love.

Occasionally, Daddy and Momma would take us for a ride after church on Sunday. We usually went to visit our relatives in Greenwood. To us, Greenwood was the city so being able to go to the city to see our cousins was always a special treat. They were usually just as excited to see us as we were to see them. When we got to Greenwood, our cousins would be waiting on the porch for us. They'd take us for a walk down the street to meet and play with some of their friends.

In addition to the good, old-fashioned fun we had riding bikes and jumping rope, our cousins always had money, and they didn't mind sharing with us. On the corner near their house was a grocery store called Joe's Market. Our cousins would always buy all types of candy and bubble gum to share with us.

Granny would fix a large meal, the smell of which summoned everyone to the dinner table to eat and fellowship. Then, after everyone was full and happy, Grandma would move the party to the front porch where the adults–Momma, Daddy, Granny, Auntie Rose, and Auntie Lizzie–would sit around and talk about the good 'ole days. Auntie Rose was very funny; she kept us laughing with her jokes. Both of our aunts live just doors apart; we enjoyed seeing and playing with our cousins.

Granny always tried to encourage Momma and Daddy to move to Greenwood, but her persuasions fell on deaf ears. After all, Daddy didn't want to live in the city.

We would hate having to come back home. For one reason, among others, Granny and Auntie Lizzie had box fans. They would sit one box fan in each window to direct the air from outside into the house. The air was never cold, but it was just enough to keep us satisfied in the hot Mississippi summer.

During the summer, Mississippi seemed to be one of the hottest places in the world, and during the winter, the coldest. We didn't have an air conditioner or even a box fan. To keep cool, we'd to fan ourselves to sleep at night using a piece of cardboard.

Summer nights seemed so long, and the heat made them absolutely miserable. We couldn't wait for daylight to appear. None of us had our own bed, so with three or four of us packed together like a can of sardines, the sweat from our warm bodies seemed to cause our skin to stick together. We slept with the windows open, trying to get any breeze that decided to come by for the evening.

If the heat wasn't enough, the constant pestering of mosquitoes simply added to our misery. All night we fought to keep the mosquetoes away, but our efforts were always to no avail. We'd wake up with bites and red spots covering our bodies.

Sometimes the bites would cause us to swell and run low-grade fevers. Every night, Momma rubb-ed us down with ointment and sprayed the whole house with mosquito repellant. After a while, it seemed as though the mosquitoes had become immune to the repellant.

When the conversation went silent, we would just sit and watch the cars and people going home from a hard day's work. Some people were going out to party or on a date with someone special for the evening, but not us, we usually stayed at home, enjoying one another.

We'd sit around for hours laughing at Daddy's jokes. His best material was the stories he told us about Uncle Wilber and Grandpa Henry.

"Henry a big talker, but you know how to shut him up?" he'd joke, "Go get Mr. Bill! Henry be shakin' in his boots when he see Mr. Bill comin' toward him."

We'd all burst out in laughter.

Daddy was always trying to dance, but he didn't have any rhythm, and he was stiff as a board. He would stand up and start to sway as if he were really about to get down, only to start stomping his foot and shaking his behind. We couldn't contain our laughter watching Daddy flail his arms and shuffle about the porch.

During the winter, our nightly shows moved from the front porch to the living room. Daddy would build a fire, and we'd sit around it, telling stories and listening to daddy's jokes just as we had done throughout the summer.

One night, in trying to stir the fire with the fire iron, sparks flew up momma's hand, causing her to say one of her chosen words. Daddy almost fell from his chair; he laughed so hard. It seemed as though the funniest moments involved Momma nearly hurting herself, like the time she stepped out onto the back porch and because of the ice on the steps, she slipped, her head hitting every step on her way down. She had a few bruises, but the only thing that was seriously hurt was her pride.

CHAPTER 7

FAMILIES HELPING FAMILIES

People who lived in Sunnyside were always helpful to one another, especially our parents. Whether someone needed a cup of cornmeal for dinner or a ride to town, Momma and Daddy always found it in their hearts to help, and their helpfulness was always returned to them. If Daddy's car broke down and he had to work on it, he didn't have to ask anyone for help.

Most of the farm workers lived close by. They could look down the road and if they saw the hood of a neighbor's car up, they didn't hesitate to walk their way to see if they needed help. Then, Daddy used that same car to help others. Daddy would take carloads of people to Greenwood on Saturdays to do their shopping or visit family, but of course, Daddy used the time to get a drink or two with the guys.

Daddy wasn't the only one who offered his car to help transport those without, and transportation wasn't the only thing shared. People shared what nature offered freely–fruits, vegetables, meats, and dairy products, amongst other necessities.

In the early fall, every family set aside time to go cut and hall firewood for the upcoming winter months. All the men would get together with their saws and axes to go cut and hall wood. Every family needed wood in order to keep warm and to cook in the wood-burning stoves and fireplaces.

When the weather was rainy and cold during the winter months, the men couldn't work in the fields or around the shop. They would get together in teams and go cut and hall wood for their families. They'd hook up mules to their wagons and be off to gather wood from the early morning to the late in the evening. The men brought back loads of wood and each family got their share of wood. They'd do this for weeks until everyone got enough wood to carry them through the cold months.

When the men came back with the wood, they'd unload it on the "woodpile." Every day during the winter, we had to go out to the woodpile to saw and cut wood. After we cut up the wood, we would bring it and stack it on the front porch against the wall of the house. Every house on the plantation had the same system for having access to their firewood. Whenever more wood was needed for the fireplace or heater, all we had to do was walk outside the front door and grab an arm full of wood for the fire. Often, the wood would be wet or have ice on it, but we still threw it on the fire and in minutes, it would be burning with a mighty flame.

Doing good deeds for one another was part of Sunnyside's culture. When people were bogged down in the depths of despair, they pulled together to lend a helping hand in whatever way they could.

They knew how to share their love, strength and support with those around them. We saw our fair share of quarrels, but any animosities between people would be forgotten and forgiven over time.

The closeness of the Sunnyside community resembled that of a family. Even discipline was a joint responsibility among community members. If an adult had to spank someone else's child, that child would be in big trouble when their parents got wind of it, no questions asked. Since parents didn't ask any questions regarding the details of their child being disciplined, we'd sometimes be falsely accused, and we never got the chance to defend ourselves.

Mr. Grayson was a grumpy old man who lived down the road from us. He grew the largest and most beautiful looking watermelons and cantaloupes, but he also thought he was the only one that did. He accused everyone of stealing his melons. One summer, he told Daddy he suspected me and my siblings to be the culprits behind his missing melons. Daddy didn't believe him, but Momma, on the other hand, was ready to lay each of us out one by one until Daddy convinced her otherwise. We didn't steal Mr. Grayson's melons that time, but later that summer, Anita devised a plan to steal one of Mr. Grayson's watermelons. I didn't want to steal that old man's melon, but Anita was in charge, so we all just followed along.

"Since he wanna accuse us of stealing his melons," she said, "We gonna give him something to tell Momma and Daddy."

That day, we ate well, and I had to admit that the sweetest watermelons were stolen ones.

In the winter was the hog slaughter. Daddy would always put several of his hogs on the fatten floor. On the fatten floor, farmers separated the hogs that would be killed from the other hogs. They were fed special grain in order to get them fat and healthy for slaughter.

I hated slaughter day. I couldn't stand the sight of Daddy killing poor little helpless animals in cold blood. I was too young to really understand that killing the poor hogs was necessary to have food that would help to feed us through the cold winter months.

On slaughter day, everyone wanted a piece of the hog, whether it was pig ears, pig tails, ham, chitterlings, lard, cracklings, or sausage. There was meat available for all of the helpers and plenty left for the owner. Even the hooves from the hog toes were used to make tea for coughs and colds, and the head was used to make hog head souse. All the hog organs and body parts were put to use in some type of way; every part was of necessity.

* * *

Men never just sat around doing absolutely nothing. They took advantage of every opportunity to make good use of their time. They would get together and go hunting, another way of putting meat on their families' tables. They usually hunted birds, rabbits, squirrels, and deer, but whatever crossed their paths was up for grabs. If one of them didn't kill much, they would share what they had with each other so that everyone went home with something in their sack.

Mrs. Mila was one of the most helpful women in Sunnyside, and everyone knew her well. She worked as a housekeeper for Mr. Webber, one of the landowners. Mrs. Mila would help anyone in whatever way necessary. She always helped our family in our most desperate times. For instance, she would give Momma money to buy us shoes and clothes throughout the year.

Whenever we needed clothes or food, Momma would write a note and leave it on Mrs. Mila's car. When Mrs. Mila got the note off of her car, she would stop by our house to see exactly what it was Momma needed, and she would bring it to Momma with promptness. Most times, Mrs. Mila brought more than what we needed.

Everyone loved Mrs. Mila because she was so kindhearted. She had an abundance of love and compassion for everyone around her. Her husband, Mr. Silas, and Daddy were good friends. They would go hunting and fishing together and hang out on the weekend, drinking beer and gambling. Every time you saw Mr. Silas, he had a mouth full of tobacco with brown juice running down his chin.

* * *

The women in Sunnyside would come together and make homemade quilts. They would sew for days and weeks, making beautiful block colorful quilts. The women would sew small pieces of material together to make one large pattern. They called it patch work quilting, and it took a great amount of time to complete one quilt, even with help. Once they finished the pattern, they would stuff the inside of the quilt with cotton or old worn out clothes. Sometimes the quilts would be so heavy that we could barely turn over in the bed when we laid underneath them.

The women also knitted and crocheted, making lovely dollies and art pieces to place on their furniture. Every time the women got together, they made and created the most magnificent articles, like homemade soap from lye and leftover cooking fats. Lye was used for a lot of things like washing clothes, dishes, and floors. It was even used for poison ivy breakouts and bug bites.

THE SUNNYSIDE STORY

As children, we knew how to get out of sight when "grown folk" got together, but that didn't mean we weren't listening. My sisters and I would sit in our bedroom next to Momma's room, where she and her friends were gathered.

The sound of their laughter always sparked a curiosity in me. I longed to know what they could have possibly been talking about. So, I would tip closer to the door and softly pressed my ear against it. With the number of times I listened in on those women's convers-ations, my ear should have made an imprint in the wood. The more I listened, the better it got.

Momma didn't party, but she would listen and laugh at the other women as they talked about their Saturday nights.

"Chile," one of the women would start, "You shoulda' seen me last night. I had on a little red skirt that stopped right at my knees and a split that went all the way up my thigh, Chile."

The women would stamp their feet and clap their hands, which seemed to encourage the woman to go on with her story.

"I couldn't keep the men off me!" she'd squeal. "And you know the main one that was trying to get a dance?"

The room would fall silent, and the suspense would nearly kill me!

"Who? Who?!" I'd think to myself, praying that none of the women could hear my thoughts screaming to know who was trying to get a dance.

After a few moments of silence, she'd say, "Mr. Grant Thomas himself."

I could hear the air being sucked out of the room with the women's collective gasp.

"Now, I know you lyin!'" one of the women would interject, "Majorie'shusban'?" she'd ask.

"Yes, ma'am. Right han' to God," the storyteller would reassure the women.

Someone in the group always had a story of dancing with someone else's husband. I wanted so badly to hollow through the door hole and ask, "Which one of you hussies was dancin' with my daddy?" but I always managed to keep my composure. However, daddy was not a dancer at all.

When I heard one of those wooden chairs make a scrubbing sound on the plank floor, I'd scurry off. That sound let me know that one of the women was scooting back in her chair to get up for something.

The women used the times they came together as both a time to create but also as an opportunity to laugh and talk about their problems. Their fellowships were a day of release–they released the stress and anxieties of living in poverty where racism covered them like a veil. The women would sit for hours, laughing and talking as they worked.

CHAPTER 8

LIVING IN THE COUNTRY

Everyone who lived in the country lived simple lives. We didn't have all of the amenities that people in the city enjoyed, but we were content. In the summer, we played with neighbors and walked the hot roads without shoes. We made playhouses with invisible friends and picked berries from bushes alongside the road. We splashed our feet in puddles and picked up pecans that had fallen from the trees. There was always a way to occupy our time. We had very little, but very little was all that we needed.

Momma knew how to make delicious homemade pies from scratch. Her pie crust shells would be light and flaky. She also made butter rolls, which was one of my favorites. When people back in the days cooked, everything was fresh and made with all-natural ingredients. They used fresh milk and butter from the cows on the farm and fresh eggs from the chickens they raised. Mostly everything was homemade or home-grown.

Our finances were limited. We couldn't afford to buy and eat junk food regularly, so it was a treat to go to the store and get a nickel or dime worth of candy or cookies. Most of the time, we drank water with our meals. We didn't know what having a cold soda felt like, but we had Kool-Aid or butter milk from the neighbor's cows on rare and special occasions. Sometimes Momma would make "sweeten water," a water and sugar mix with a few drops of vinegar or lemon juice for flavoring.

* * *

My parents would occasionally entertain guests at our house. Family members or friends would come spent the night with us. Whenever they did, someone had to give up their bed and sleep on the floor. Momma would make a pallet, layering quilts or blankets on the hard, wooden floor to make it as comfortable as she could, which was never comfortable enough. We didn't have many quilts and blankets to start with, so the cover Momma put on the floor to make the pallet would be too thin. We never had an overflow of anything so having to share our bed covers with guests was an inconvenience, to say the least. Although we enjoyed having family and friends spend the night with us from time to time, having to share our limited blankets and quilts made their visits a little less enjoyable.

Living in the country and working on the plantation taught us endurance. Not everyone was made to live the country life let alone work in the field. Real country folks were rough and tough. They were strong and determined. You had to be strong in order to survive the rigors of farming and raising children with very little resources. Every day was a new challenge.

People from the city looked down on people from the country. The way most country folks talked, people assumed they were uneducated and dumb, which was far from the truth. We had southern accents and we were country to the bone, but we were far from dumb.

Momma did all that she could to ensure that we didn't sound unlearned. She was intentional about instilling in us the idea that we should present ourselves in a way so that no one would be mistaken about how intelligent we were. She wanted us to speak well, but she also taught us not to be ashamed of our southern drawl.

"You gotta carry yourself in the best way you can," momma would say, "You gotta be the best you can be by always reachin' high and not settlin' for jus anything." The sky is the limit."

Back then, parents didn't see a problem with keeping their children out of school to work in the fields. So, most children graduated from high school much later than they should have or quit school altogether to work.

Even we missed school many days to help our parents work in the field. Denise, our oldest sister, had to quit school at an early age to work and help support our family. Later on, Anita dropped out of school to work too. I never dropped out, but I missed countless days of school to babysit while Momma, Daddy, Anita, and Denise worked in the fields. I never expressed how staying at home to babysit bothered me, but I wanted to go to school with the rest of my friends, and sometimes, I didn't have that luxury.

Sometimes, working in the fields appeared to be the number one priority for many parents. Our daddy never finished school, so to him, dropping out of school to work in the fields wasn't a big deal. Daddy never had a problem with us missing school. Had it not been for

Momma, we would have never even gone to school. On cold and rainy days, Daddy always tried to persuade Momma to let us stay home from school.

"Them kids too small to go out in that kinda weather," he'd plead, but Momma wouldn't budge.

I thank God for Momma, having enough sense to know that we needed to be in school.

* * *

People in the city always labeled Southerners as "country folk." Most of us didn't have a problem with being called country, but trouble was subject to brew if someone called you dumb or stupid, then you had a problem on your hands. Most city people would laugh and make fun of the way Southerners talked, but regardless of our dialects, the conversations we had with one another were always genuine.

Chapter 9

THE PLANTATION WORKERS

Every plantation had a straw boss. The straw boss was like the landowner's assistant. Whatever the boss wanted done, he would relay the message to the straw boss for the other farm workers to get the job done. Daddy was the straw boss on the Sunnyside plantation for many years, but Daddy never liked being in charge. It wasn't in him to have to tell others what to do.

Daddy's reluctance to being the straw boss was further agitated by the fact that he was good friends with most, if not all, of the other workers, but Mr. Bill asked Daddy and Daddy didn't say no, probably out of fear that there was really no other option. At times, Daddy being the straw boss caused a lot of conflict between him and the other workers. Being the straw boss didn't mean you made more money than the other workers or had special privileges.

It simply meant that you had more responsibilities. Sometimes other workers would call Daddy a "do boy" or a "flunky." Daddy didn't like trouble with anyone, but I could tell those names made him angry, despite how peaceful a person he was.

One time, Daddy and Grandpa Henry got into an altercation when Daddy was trying to tell Grandpa Henry where Mr. Bill wanted him to work for the day.

"You a big fat lie, Willie!" Grandpa Henry said, "Ain't nobody tol' me to do nothin' so that jus' what I'm gon' do!"

Daddy kept his composure for a few minutes, but he couldn't keep his composure anymore after a while.

"If you don't wanna do it, then you can take that up with Mr. Bill," Daddy said, looking Henry straight in the eyes.

Grandpa Henry's fear of Mr. Bill was just enough to put him in his place.

Plantation workers dedicated their lives to working on the farm, and their work ethics were incomparable. By not working hard, they knew what was at risk: the survival and support of their families. The landowners knew their workers were dedicated and hardworking; they didn't show much love or respect for them.

Most of the workers wanted a change for a better life. The money they made was just enough to feed their families, and sometimes not even that. They knew living on the plantation would never present them with the chance to mobilize, but they never gave up.

* * *

When we were done working in the field, the household still had to be done, but most of the time, Momma and Daddy's pay schedules didn't align with our chore schedules. In order to buy soap, Momma and Daddy would have to wait until the weekend to get paid. I remember Momma washing our clothes late at night and hanging them out to dry in the dark.

Women had to wash clothes by hand and hang the clothes outside on the clothesline. Everyone had a homemade clothesline made out of twine, rope, cord, or barb wire. The clothesline needed a prop to support it, placed in the middle to balance out the weight of wet clothes. Depending on the length of the clothesline, several props were used to support the line. The prop was just a long, heavy piece of wood or pipe.

The women would make a fire under a big, black, iron wash pot and let the water come to a boil. We never had a real clothes basket to carry our clothes to the line. We would use a crate or a bushel basket, which was used for picking fruits and vegetables. We would always run out of clothes pins and have to hang some of our clothes on the barb wire fence. Momma would fuss at us about snatching the clothes from the line because it would cause the clothes pins to pop and break. The clothes pins that Momma could afford were made from a thin, yellow natural bamboo wood.

Momma was very particular about her clothes. We couldn't just hang out her laundry any kind of way. We had to categorize our clothes—all the whites were hung first, then the light colors, and lastly, the dark colors were hung together. Not only did they have to be hung according to color, but by article—shirts were hung from the bottom and pants were hung from the waist. Every piece of clothing had to be hung the way Momma wanted them hung, or she would snatch them all down and make us start all over.

On Saturday, the women would sometimes wash all day because everyone had huge families. They would have tons of dirty clothes to wash by hand. When Monday morning rolled around, all the men would be clean and fresh ready for work.

* * *

While the women tended to the household chores on the weekends, the men would party and drink. After a long week of working on the plantation, it seemed as though the men had something to celebrate.

After leaving the corner store just after dark, the men would get together and trail each other to another location to finish off the night. Many of them should have been going home, but they chose to continue on their drinking adventures, always ending up in a place called Minter City, which wasn't too far from Sunnyside.

They loved going to the juke houses, which were nothing more than night clubs and bars. They would hang out all night long. Many times, the juke house was someone's home or some kind of small shack far out in the country back in the woods. The owner of the juke house would sell liquor and food.

People were also allowed to gamble. The men would shoot dice for money. The gambling would go on late into the night and early morning. The men didn't have a lot of money to begin with, but they took their chances. The men would win large sums of money, but sometimes they lost most or all of their money and would be scared to go home.

Many times the gambling would cause terrible altercations among the men and fights would break out without notice. Every weekend someone was getting shot or cut over gambling.

In the juke house was a large music box that sat in the corner of the room. They called it a "See Burg" back in the days. It costed a nickel to play a song. The See Burg could be heard from miles away, and it had a large selection of all kind of songs. Anything you wanted to hear was in the See Burg. On any given night, the See Burg could be found playing the Blues.

During the week, the workers would slave their lives away working in the fields from sunup to sundown. Throughout the week, they kept their feelings inside, but as soon as Saturday evening rolled around and they got a few cans of beer in their bellies, all of the frustrations that they were holding in during the week came to a boil.

All hell would break loose. Their emotions would take over and things got out of control. They would all meet up at the corner store with anger and frustration from the week built up in their hearts and minds.

Sunnyside residents loved one another but working on the plantation together caused a lot of tension between neighbors, friends, and even families. They would start arguing and fussing about the simplest issues. It seemed as though alcohol helped them bring out what they really wanted to say to one another. Depending on the subject of the argument, some verbal altercations resulted in physical altercations, some going as far as stabbing, cutting, and even shooting.

When Mrs. Bertha found out her husband, Mr. Tom was having an affair with her best friend, a shootout ensued. Everyone knew about the affair, but Mrs. Berta. When Mr. Tom started getting a little relaxed, being seen around Sunnyside with his mistress, the situation ran out of control.

Cheating and wrongdoing were common on the plantations. Even the landowners were involved in messing around with the workers' wives and girlfriends. I once heard Daddy telling Momma about one of the landowners, Mr. John, having an affair with one of the young girls on the plantation.

Every weekend something was bound to happen once the men got liquor in them. It never failed. We would be out in our front yard or just sitting on the porch minding our own business when a round of bullets would start flying. Momma would make us run in the house and stay down until the shooting settled down. The police weren't called unless someone was killed, but the confrontations hardly ever got to that point.

The women on the plantation had their issues too, which were usually even more extreme than the men's. It seemed as though the women could create situations from a dust particle. When young women would get into arguments, it was never just them, but their mothers always got involved. Now, you talking about a good mess! The way small conflicts would spin out of control always made for some great entertainment.

When Betsy and Sarah finally found out they were both dating the same man, they decided to meet up to hash out the situation. Their meetup started as a conversation, but they were fighting like cats and dogs in minutes, beating each other down. Eventually, Bob, the shared man, showed up. Witnesses say that Bob told them that he didn't care who won; he didn't want either of them.

Quarrels between married couples were just as common as quarrels between unmarried couples. Husbands and wives would break up on the weekend, but by the end of the next week, they'd be back together in one home.

Plantation workers would fuss and fight among each other and kept the mess going throughout the entire weekend. Yet, regardless of what Mr. Bill said or did to them, they wouldn't lift an eyebrow to defend themselves. No matter what the problem was or how bad it had gotten, they were able to hold their peace and move on when their issue was one with Mr. Bill.

Just as Mr. Bill knew everything that happened on his plantation, he knew everything that happened in Sunnyside. When Monday morning rolled around, Mr. Bill would somehow always know who "shot John." Someone was always telling Mr. Bill about everything that had taken place over the weekend. Mr. Bill acted as if he were Justice of the Peace. He'd fuss and curse at the workers who were in a mess over the weekends and order them to straighten up.

Some of the workers had it bad about being snitches, telling on other workers, but of all of the snitches, Grandpa Henry was the worst. Henry would tell on anyone to save himself from being chastised by Mr. Bill. Henry had a habit of making up lies about different workers. He'd often tell Mr. Bill that another worker hadn't done a good job on his work or that someone was taking a break when they shouldn't have been.

Henry was notorious for sneaking around, watching other workers, and trying to find something to lie on them about. He'd go as far as taking fuel or parts from the farm equipment to make it look like someone else had tampered with it. If Henry didn't know how to do anything else, he surely knew how to stir up some trouble.

Mr. Bill didn't have a favorite, but he made certain workers believe they were to have an inside scoop on what the other workers were up to. The only concern Mr. Bill had was getting the news of what was going on. The moment you crossed the line with Mr. Bill or didn't fulfill your responsibilities for the day, you had trouble on your hands.

CHAPTER 10

HOW OUR MUM AND DAD MET

Our parents met when they were young in 1945. According to them, it was love at first sight. Daddy was born in 1925 in Silver City, Mississippi. Momma was born in Belzoni, Mississippi in 1928. Belzoni was about five miles from Silver City. A few years later, our mom's parent's relocated to Silver City, Mississippi. Momma finished school in Silver City, and they stayed there for many years.

Since our Grandma was a churchgoing woman, Momma had no choice but to be raised in the church. Back then, church was the centerpiece of the family, and everyone in the household was obligated to go.

When Momma and her family first moved to Silver City, Daddy had gone into the Army Reserve, but his time there was brief. Daddy started having medical issues and was discharged. He was sent back home to Silver City.

After returning home, Daddy decided to put together a gospel group with his only brother, Virgil, and two of his closest friends, Ray and Johnny. They began traveling, singing in different places, mostly at churches in the rural areas. Most of the time, they sang without making a dime, but that didn't stop them from singing. They were dedicated to their singing ministry.

Singing the gospel gave groups an opportunity to travel and to meet people, especially young ladies. One summer night, Daddy and his group were on a program to sing at Shiloh Baptist Church, the church Momma and her family attended.

The story goes: Momma and her family had gotten to church early and Momma was already seated. When Daddy and his group entered the church, Momma spotted him from a distance. As they began to set up their equipment, Daddy looked out into the sanctuary, and that's where he first laid eyes on Momma. He couldn't take his eyes off Momma. After seeing Momma in the congregation, Daddy and his group really put on a show! They sang the roof off the church, as the elderly folk would say.

Daddy watched mama the whole night. He couldn't wait for service to end so he could go make Momma's acquaintance. Daddy made sure that his friend Johnny or Ray didn't get to Momma before he did. Daddy didn't waste any time finding who the beautiful woman he had seen in the congregation was.

Momma and Daddy finally met, and not too long after; they began dating. One of their favorite spots was a small, country hole-in-the-wall called the Midnight Club. They would meet at the Midnight Club and stay there for hours, eating, drinking, and entertaining one another.

Only one year after meeting, in 1946, Momma was pregnant with Denise. Momma was only eighteen, and Daddy was twenty-one. So, later on that same year, Momma and Daddy decided to get married. Two years later, in 1948, Anita was born.

Momma and Daddy stayed in Silver City until Anita was about three years old. But after a while, they decided to pack up their belongings and move to the Mississippi Delta, making their home in Sunnyside.

Daddy and Momma were so in love that they had a baby almost every two years. Altogether, our parents had five daughters and two sons. My four younger siblings and I were born in Sunnyside.

Even after moving to Sunnyside and having all of their children, Daddy still managed to keep in touch with his gospel group. They'd occasionally find time to get together and perform. I can remember Daddy and his group rehearsing at our house many times. Daddy was serious about singing, so whenever a group member showed Daddy that he wasn't as serious as Daddy, Daddy had no problem with replacing him with another singer. As time passed, Daddy started slowing down with his singing, and after a while, he stopped singing altogether.

CHAPTER 11
DADDY'S STORY

Daddy's full name was Willie Jacob Tanner. Throughout our lives, Daddy showered us with love and tender care, giving us what he was able to provide. We had a home to live in, and we never went hungry. Daddy also cherished our mom. He took care of her with everything in him.

Daddy would get up all through the night to check our beds, making sure we were okay and covered up from the cold. He kept logs of wood on the fire all night to keep us warm. He would keep a bucket of water for us to drink from at night near our beds so that we didn't have to go into the cold kitchen.

Sometimes, if we got up too late and missed the school bus, Daddy would take us to school. On Sunday afternoons after church, Daddy would take us down this long, gravel road to a little country store where he would buy us candy or cookies to eat on the way home. Daddy had a lighter skin complexion, and he was sort of heavy set.

He had smooth, curly hair that was cold black. Most women considered Daddy attractive. Daddy would make waves in his hair using Murray Pomade, a thick grease, which held Daddy's hair in place for hours. If Daddy's hair didn't set him apart, his gold tooth did. Daddy kept that gold tooth shining, scrubbing it with baking soda.

Despite Daddy's looks and gold tooth, he always remained humble and kind, but he was as sneaky as could be. Denise would always see daddy with other women or at some woman's house. Somehow, he would always convince Denise not to tell Momma that she had seen him. Daddy would ride women around with him as if he were single, but he never came past our house unless it was past midnight when he knew Momma would be asleep.

Daddy took back roads to get to where he was going making sure Momma never caught him with another woman. Even though Daddy did all he could to make sure Momma never caught him, he didn't seem to mind that I and my brothers and sisters always saw him. I loved Daddy but seeing him with other women angered me to my very spirit. Still, I could never bring myself to telling Momma what I had seen.

Daddy knew he looked good, so he never had to flaunt himself around women. His calm and quiet personality attracted women like bees to honey. Whenever Daddy got around women, he had this look about him, smiling with his mouth half twisted, showing off that big gold tooth. I would watch his every move, and I came to realize that Daddy was just one big flirt.

He was also good about being the handy man, always willing to take women places they needed to go. I didn't mind Daddy helping people, but sometimes, I found him to be a little too helpful.

When we would be working out in the field, we would hear the women on the plantation whispering to each other about Daddy. The plantation women would always bring up a conversation about the men on the plantation while they would be working out in the field. Somehow, Daddy's name always came up.

Everyone seemed to have a story about how much of a good man Daddy was, but they never found a reason to share those stories with Momma. They made sure that Momma was nowhere near before they started their gossip, but they didn't seem to care about me and my siblings hearing them talk about our daddy. The stories made our blood boil, but we never confronted the storytellers, and we never told Momma.

The women were very careful and respectful toward Momma because they knew that she didn't mind speaking her mind or using her hoe. One day while working in the field, Myra began talking about what men on the plantation were good looking.

"Yeah, that Will Tanner got 'em all beat," she said, holding a mouthful of chewing tobacco in her cheeks. "That man might be the best lookin' man in Sunnyside. Boy, I'd love getting' wit him," she continued.

If looks could kill, my gaze would have been enough to bury that big woman. I watched Myra and listened as she went on and on about how handsome my daddy, but I held my tongue and kept working.

Even though no one ever told Momma about what Daddy was doing, Momma was far from a fool. Momma somehow knew how other women felt about Daddy, and she would occasionally get on to him. So, to keep Momma from fulfilling her threats, packing up her things, and leaving, Daddy became skilled in the art of lying.

Daddy and Momma would argue about Daddy's cheating. Every argument ended with Momma making threats to leave Daddy, but he somehow always knew how to talk her out of it. One time, momma went as far as to pack her belongings and set them by the front door while ordering all of us to do the same. When we were all packed and ready to go, John, one of our neighbors, was supposed to take us to the bus station.

Unbeknownst to Momma at the time, John never really intended to take her to the bus station. John was one of Daddy's best friends, and Daddy would have never forgiven him if he would have taken Momma and the seven of us to the bus station in Momma's attempt to leave Daddy.

Earlier in the week, Momma had talked to John, and he assured her that he would come and take her to the bus station that Saturday night. He told Momma that he would be there for her shortly after daddy left for the juke house, his regular Saturday ritual.

We were all packed and ready. We waited and waited for John, but he never came.

Weeks later, John apologized to Momma for lying and told her that he just couldn't do a thing like that to his friend. He was so tickled when he talked to mama because he knew that mama was going to read him his rights. He also told Momma that he and daddy were together, hanging out at the juke house the night he was supposed to take her to the station.

One afternoon, Momma was waiting on Daddy to come home to take her to the store. She waited and waited, and finally, Daddy showed up smelling like cheap perfume and looking crazy. As soon as Daddy walked through the door, Momma sprang toward him.

"Why youjus' now getting' home? Where you been Will? You knew I had some place to go!" she yelled, her face less than two inches from Daddy's.

Daddy watched Momma with a slight grin on his face. He tried to play stupid like he didn't know that he was supposed to come pick Momma up to take her to the store.

They argued for hours until Daddy finally fell asleep. Daddy didn't have to admit it, but we all knew that he had been out with his girlfriend. Daddy's boldness with his cheating was disrespectful, but he never thought to change his ways.

Sometimes, Momma would get so fed up with Daddy's mess that she'd hit him, slapping him upside the head and daring him to strike back. Even though Daddy disrespected Momma with his cheating, he never raised his hand to hit her. Daddy wasn't a fighter. He was a lover and a cheater.

* * *

Sometimes Daddy would spend too much money or gamble his money away and pretend he lost it. He would go to his car and pretend to search desperately for the money he claimed he lost. He would even have all of us helping him look for the mysterious vanishing money in the car. Momma would get so mad. She'd make us come in the house because she knew daddy was lying, knowing all along that he had spent nearly every dime he had. But he made sure he kept a small portion for himself so that he could still go out and have a good time. It was never much money because he didn't have that much extra money to begin with. Still, Momma didn't want him spending the money that she felt should have been saved. Momma knew how hard times were. After all, they had seven children to feed.

Daddy didn't like arguing, especially with Momma. When he messed up, he wouldn't say hardly anything. He'd sit by the fireplace with his arms folded across his stomach and eyes closed tight, pretending to be asleep.

He was probably thinking of how he was going to get out of his mess and get back on Momma's good side. If things got too heated, he would get up and walk outside. Daddy usually just let Momma have her say, and that's exactly what she would do. She would have her say because Daddy knew she was right about the things she accused him of doing.

Daddy's cheating and running around left him with several children outside of his marriage with Momma.

Daddy had a huge family with many siblings. They all lived up north in different states. Most of his sisters lived in St. Louis. Every other month they would call Mrs. Slawson at the corner store and leave a message for Momma to check on the family and to see if she needed anything for us.

Daddy' sisters knew the things Daddy was doing to our momma. When they finally decided that enough was enough, they began to encourage Momma to leave Daddy and move to St. Louis. They assured Momma that she could do so much better there, and they would help her get everything she needed. Momma was really close to Daddy's sister Rosemary. She always looked out for us and never failed to help with whatever we needed.

"O'Lee," Rosemary would call Momma, a shortened Ora Lee, "I'm tellin' ya, St. Louis is the place to be!" they'd tell Momma, "You can come up here and get a good-payin' job, and the kids can go to school in one of these big, nice school buildings."

The way Daddy's sisters described St. Louis made the city sound like heaven on earth. According to my aunts, the apples and oranges in St. Louis were large as our heads, and there was a store where you can get clothes and shoes for only ten cents.

During the summertime, some of my aunts would drive down to Sunnyside to visit us for a few days. Whenever they would come down to visit, they would bring us food, clothes, and shoes.

When they visited, we were always short on drinking glasses and cups. We never had nice dishes, just mason jars and cans, and we hated for guests to ask for something to drink, even though we knew they would since the heat from the Sunnyside summer could draw water out of you like a well. It never failed; as soon as our aunts would arrive and sit down for a few minutes, they would ask for a glass of water. We would be so embarrassed; we would start to look at one another to see who was going into the kitchen to get the water.

When I was chosen to fetch the water, I would purposely stay in the kitchen as long as I could, hoping that our aunts would forget about the water, but they never forgot.

"Where dat water at, gyal?" one of them would call to the kitchen. After looking for mason jars to no avail, I would put the water in tin cans and take it to them. They never seemed to have a problem with drinking from the tin can.

Our aunts tried their hardest to make Momma believe that St Louis was the best place to be if she desired to have a prosperous life. They painted a picture like mama could get government assistance for us over night.

"You could even get your own house, fully furnished," Nellie prodded.

The seven of us would listen to our aunt's stories of St. Louis and be happy as clams at the thought of moving to such a wonderful place. We took everything our aunts said as true, but Momma knew that much of what they said was nothing more than an exaggeration. Momma had been married into Daddy's family for many years; she knew all about their character. Momma knew how they exaggerated everything, and just like Daddy, lied like rugs.

"My sisters are just big 'ole liars, and the truth ain't in 'em," Daddy would say when he would get wind of his sisters trying to convince Momma to leave him and move with them to St. Louis.

We kept waiting and waiting for Momma to make her move, but she never did. I would be watching to see if she was packing up stuff for us to go, but she never did.

One time, Aunt Nellie decided to write Momma a long letter telling her how great St. Louis was. Daddy could barely read, but he always managed to figure things out, like when the mail that came to the house was from out of state. When Daddy saw the piece of mail from aunt Nellie, he knew that it was from St. Louis. Daddy waited until Momma wasn't home and had Denise to read the letter to him. Denise was a daddy's girl, so she didn't hesitate when Daddy asked her to read the letter to him.

"Dear O'Lee," Denise read, "I hope you in better spirits than the last time we talked. I know you say you not tryin' to come to St. Louis, but I'm sure if you came, you won't regret it."

Daddy listened intently as Denise read the letter in its entirety. It said the same things that Daddy's sisters had been trying to convince Momma of for months–St. Louis is the most wonderful place to be, and the streets were lined with gold.

"There should be a bus leaving from Mississippi to St. Louis soon; you should try to catch it. Don't worry about bringin' nothin' with you. Everything you need we can get when you get here," Denise continued. "I love my brother, but that man ain'tgon' never change, O' Lee."

Daddy had heard enough.

When Momma came home, Daddy was furious. He told Momma everything that was in the letter, and the greatest argument that they ever had ensued.

"You can believe them women if you want," he argued, the veins in his neck bulging, "but I told you, they aintnothin' but liars! You move to St. Louis, and you gone be all by yo'self!"

As the argument died down, Daddy reverted back to his usual act, persuading Momma not to leave. Daddy had a way of making up with Momma and getting things back right.

Daddy did everything in his power to get back on Momma's good side. He would treat Momma so kindly. He'd take her on a ride to town, usually to go get ice cream or a cold soda. He'd whisper in Momma's ear, and with a slight smile, she would push him away. Daddy would grab a chair, sit beside Momma, and lightly rub her back.

Momma would always act tough and mean when she was angry, but Daddy always found a way to tear down her wall. Daddy really did love our momma, but he took things too far.

They would eventually make up and straighten things out for a while, but Daddy was always watching to make sure Momma wasn't packing up her clothes. Even after the letter incident passed, Momma was suspicious of how Daddy could have possibly known what the letter said, knowing Daddy couldn't read. Then, one day, she thought to ask Denise.

"You remember that letter from your Aunt Nellie?" Momma asked Denise.

Denise began to fidget and look every which way but at Momma. She knew what she had done. Denise was sweating like a sinner in church. She was scared of what Momma would do after finding out that it was she who had read Daddy the letter, but she was even more scared to lie to our Momma.

"Yes ma'am," Denise said, her voice shaking and eyes swelling with tears.

"Did you read that letter to your Daddy?" Momma continued.

The tears in her eyes continued to form.

"Yes ma'am," Denise answered hesitantly.

Momma sat back in her chair and watched Denise, who stood stoically waiting to see what Momma would say.

"Alright baby, you can go," Momma said, leaning up in her chair while puffing on her Pall Mall cigarette.

Momma wasn't upset at Denise for reading Daddy the letter, but she was furious that Daddy brought Denise in the middle of their issues. Over time, Momma got over the letter situation. When Daddy wasn't around, she'd make jokes and laugh at the fact that Daddy needed Denise to read the letter.

* * *

Daddy was a patient and peaceful man. It took quite a bit to get under his skin, but when something did, you had trouble on your hands. I remember once Daddy got upset with Mr. Bill and came home early from working the field. For daddy to leave work and come home, he had to be really angry. Daddy had realized that he had been being cheated of his pay.

"I'm not going back out there until Mr. Bill get my money right," he told Momma, pacing around the living room, sweat dripping down his face.

Daddy didn't have much of an education, but he could count his money and keep track of his pay. He had spoken to Mr. Bill on several occasions about the hours he had worked, but somehow, Mr. Bill failed to follow up on it. When Daddy decided to talk to Mr. Bill about his money again to tell Mr. Bill that his pay wasn't right and that he owed him more money, Mr. Bill kept promising Daddy that he would straighten out the misunderstanding, but he never did.

Daddy left that field and didn't work for several days. When Mr. Bill realized that Daddy wasn't coming back to plow his cotton until he got his rightful pay, he came to the house looking for Daddy. He apologized for the mistake and paid Daddy every dime he owed him. Daddy went back to work the next day.

* * *

Growing up, the seven of us went to Daddy with our problems because he was gentle and knew how to get his point across with very few words. When we got in trouble, we wanted Daddy to deal with us. Momma quickly wanted to whip us, but Daddy talked to us and explained why what we did was wrong. Daddy would threaten to whip us, but he never brought himself to actually do it.

One time I and my younger siblings, decided to help Momma with chores by washing for her. Momma always warned against us using Clorox, but when we decided to surprise her, her warning was forgotten. We put a load of clothes in the washing pot and doused them with Clorox. When the clothes were done, we hung them on the line.

Momma came home to see a rainbow of spotted clothes hanging up to dry, and since no one asked us to do the clothes and we ruined them, Momma was furious. Every one of us got a whipping that day.

He had a different way of disciplining us.

If Daddy had one rule, it was to stay away from his fishing poles. One time, I decided to use Daddy's pole to play a game with some dogs that came around our house. I got one of Daddy's fishing poles and climbed to the top of the car that was parked in our yard. I called the dogs to the car and began poking them with the pole, trying to make them angry.

As I poked at one of the dogs, the fishing pole got stuck on one of the dog's collars. Snap! The pole broke in two. I quickly jumped down from the car and ran around to the back of the house to put the fishing pole back where I found it.

I waited for Momma and Daddy to come home and braced myself for my punishment. Daddy saw his broken fishing pole and asked if I had broken it.

"Yes sir," I said.

"Now what I told y'all about messing with my fishing poles?" he asked.

Daddy was angry. He pulled me close to him and looked me straight in the eyes.

"Gal, this is my last time warning you. Don't ever mess with my poles again," he said.

On Saturday nights, Daddy would put on his starched khaki pants and go out to the town, but he wore his Sunday's best with pride on Sunday mornings. On any day of the week, Daddy could care less about dressing with style. As long as he had a pair of old boots with no strings, a pair of overalls, a plaid shirt, and a cap, he was good to go.

Daddy would get a haircut every few weeks for twenty-five cents. He shaved weekly and shined his gold tooth.

Daddy enjoyed going hunting. He would take our two yard dogs, Whitey and Brownie, out hunting with him, but he was so tickled at the fact that those dogs were the sorriest hunting dogs you'd ever see. Every time he fired a shot, the dogs would howl in fear. They never even chased a single rabbit.

He didn't engage in conversations concerning negative things or talking about other people. He would always listen to what others had to say, but he wouldn't say a word if their conversations were filled with negativity. Daddy didn't like mess and gossip. He didn't have much input when people wanted to share information about other peoples' affairs. Unfortunately, plantation workers always kept gossip going.

When one of Daddy's friends, who wanted to leave his wife for a younger woman, wanted Daddy's opinion on what he should do, it didn't take long for him to realize that daddy wasn't the one he needed to be talking to.

Daddy didn't have any comments or concerns for other peoples' business, and he tried to teach us to be the same way.

"Keep your mouths closed and don't to get in other folk business," he'd say.

Despite Daddy's shortcomings, especially with his infidelity, he was a wonderful father who always made sure that Momma and his children were taken care of. He didn't have much of an education, but he was an excellent farmer and an even better handyman. He plowed and made rows of cotton so neat and straight. He worked with farming machinery like none other and worked on cars like a professional mechanic, putting new motors in his car and replacing old tired breaks with new ones. Daddy wasn't blessed with a formal schooling, but what he lacked in the area of schooling, he made up for with his practical knowledge.

* * *

In the spring, Daddy and Momma would plant a huge garden. The garden would be filled with greens, beans, peas, okra, tomatoes, corn and much more. We always had plenty of vegetables. People back in the days would call a large garden a "truck patch." Just before the winter set in, we would have to gather the peanuts, sweet potatoes, and everything else we had left in the garden. Our parents not only planted in the spring but at the end of summer, they planted seeds again for winter vegetables. We had collard greens, turnips, mustard greens, potatoes, and peanuts. The winter vegetables always tasted better because of the frost. The frost would fall on the vegetables and make them tender and sweet.

After the winter set in and all of the food from the garden had been harvested, the truck patch would turn into our play area. During the winter, the huge plot of land would freeze over and turn into a solid sheet of thick ice. We used the plot as a skating rink. We'd play on the ice for hours.

Along with Daddy being a great hunter and fisherman, he raised hogs and chickens. He did whatever it took to keep food on our table year-round. During the late fall season when the harvesting was over and the winter made it too cold for Daddy to work out in the fields, he would get up and get dressed, put on his big, green army coat and his steel toe boots, and gather his hunting gear to go hunting.

I loved to eat, but I hated when I saw Daddy preparing to go hunting because I knew that whatever he got, I would be the one left to clean it. When Daddy went hunting, he'd always catch wild rabbits and squirrels. He'd bring a sack full of them home, and I would stand in the cold cleaning every last one of the animals from Daddy's sack, or at least that was expected of me. I didn't have the patience to clean all of the squirrels and rabbits that Daddy had killed, especially the ones that had been torn to pieces by the bullet. So, I would clean one or two and throw one or two right down the Tallahatchie River. Clean one or two more. Throw one or two more down the river. I did this until Daddy's hunting sack was empty. Then, I'd take the cleaned venison into the house for Daddy to inspect.

"Gyal, I thought I had more rabbits than that," Daddy would say, surprised at how few squirrels or rabbits I had cleaned.

I always managed to reassure him that the hair on the animals probably gave off the illusion that he had captured more squirrels or rabbits than he actually had. I knew I was lying, but I didn't even care because I refused to stand in the freezing cold all day cleaning some smelly animals.

I was always a picky eater. Usually, I was okay with eating whatever Momma had prepared, but when she would cook the same thing over and over again, I just couldn't do it. I would be so upset about having to eat greens or soup every day that I would pout and go sit on the porch, just waiting for Momma to come after me and ask me what was wrong. I was fearful to tell Momma what was wrong, but I always managed to muster up the courage to tell her that I didn't want to eat what she had prepared. Momma didn't force anyone to eat, so she would just let me be. I would sit on the porch, waiting for Daddy to get off his tractor to ask if I could go to the store to get something to eat since I didn't want what Momma cooked. He'd hesitate for a minute, but he'd always let me go.

"Go on and tell Alice to give you what you want," he'd say.

Daddy had an account at the store, and Mrs. Slawson never had a problem letting me get what I wanted because she knew that Daddy would pay her. Daddy was dependable. He never skipped out on paying his debts.

By the time Daddy finished his sentence, I'd already be halfway to the Slawson's store.

I would get a six-cent soda, fifteen cents worth of cookies, which were two for a penny, and about twenty-five cents worth of bologna. The Slawson's store had the best bologna in the world.

I'd walk into the store and Mrs. Slawson would be smiling with a shiny gold tooth showing on the side of her mouth.

"How yadoin', Little Bit," she'd ask, as the bell hanging atop of the door jangled above me.

"I'm fine," I'd say, making my way through the store and ending up at the front counter, arms filled with snacks and goodies, "Can I get some bologna?"

"Ok baby," she'd say, grabbing a roll of bologna out of the refrigerator and taking it to the slicer.

I'd watch her set up the machine and place the bologna on top of it with amazement. She'd lay a thin sheet of wax paper on the counter just under the machine's blade to catch the falling meat. Then when she was finished with her set up, she'd wipe down the blade with a white rag and place the roll of bologna perfectly near the blade's edge on the meat tray.

Mrs. Slawson always knew how to slice my bologna just how I liked it, and the smell of the bologna put me in a trance. While Mrs. Slawson sliced, she'd ask me how Momma and Daddy was and how I was doing in school. I'd answer, but my eyes stayed fixed on the meat that fell onto the wax paper.

After cutting about six or seven slices, Mrs. Slawson would neatly fold the wax paper over the bologna and place it in a brown paper sack. She'd smile and hand me the sack over the counter and compliment me with a cookie for my walk home.

"Go straight home, and be careful going down that road," she'd say, sending me off with a sack full of snacks and a free cookie.

I always made sure that I got enough to share with my brothers and sisters. They'd be ecstatic to see me walk in the house with a sack full of junk food since we rarely had junk food, and there were never snacks in the house.

Coming back from the store, I would always walk extremely slowly, especially if it wasn't dark yet. I would be trying to buy time, preparing myself for what Momma was going to say when she saw me with a bag full of snacks after I didn't eat her food. Usually, she would fuss at daddy for letting me go, but he never really paid much attention to her fussing.

* * *

During certain years, Momma and Daddy would sharecrop. A landowner would allow poor farmers to use a portion of his land to raise crops, and in return, the landowners could sell the rest of the crops. Cotton was one of the only crops that would generate cash for the sharecroppers. Farmers used the sharecropping system to pay off debts that had accrued and made a little bit of money with only a small amount to invest initially.

Most of the farmers that worked as sharecroppers went into debt buying supplies from the landowner. They not only needed money for supplies, but they also needed help providing for themselves and their families until harvest time. The sharecroppers' crops were all they had to offer for collateral.

Sharecroppers' profits were usually slim, which meant that their debt was growing larger and larger. Sinking deeper into debt, their only option was to sign on as a sharecropper for another year. Year after year, farmers would try to sharecrop their way out of debt, but unless their earnings at the end of the year were greater than their debt, they'd be stuck in the seemingly endless cycle of sharecropping.

If by chance the farmer made a profit that year, he'd get a bonus. The bonus was never much, usually only enough to pay off other debts like the farmer's commissary account. Throughout the year, farmers purchased goods from the commissary store, which was owned by the landowner.

The commissary sold shoes, clothes, tools, food, pretty much anything you needed. Families would go to the commissary to shop and put the entire purchase on their bill. Unfortunately, the prices at the commissary were so outrageous that regularly purchasing simple necessities had the power to drive a family so far into debt that it had no chance of getting out of debt that year. By keeping farmers in debt, landowners kept them under his feet. Landowners had no pity for the poor. The farmer's debt was the landowner's first priority, and with any money that the farmers made, they made sure their money came off the top.

Some families were day workers. Day workers would work on one field, and when the work was done on that field, they'd be off to the next field. Unlike farm workers, day workers got paid every day. Farm workers had to wait until the weekend to be paid.

My parents and older siblings worked hard all year, and at the end of the year, just before Christmas, we would be waiting and hoping that Daddy came back with money from sharecropping. That was the only way we would be able to get gifts for Christmas. When Daddy would walk through the door, we could tell by the look on his face when all of their work only resulted in breaking even. More often than not, we always broke even. I never actually believed that the debt Mr. Bill said we owed was the correct amount. It was just another way to get over on the poor, Black man to keep him on the plantation forever.

The seven of us were sad for a while, knowing we wouldn't be getting clothes or toys that Christmas, but Momma and Daddy would go into the room and have a one-on-one talk, which always seemed to result in us having a great Christmas dinner days later. Daddy would have borrowed money all over again just so we could have food for Christmas.

Despite our disappointment about not getting any gifts, Momma always knew how to cheer us up. When we saw the cakes, pies, apples, oranges, and peppermint candy, the sadness of not getting toys slipped away. It never took much to make us happy. As long as we had food and one another for Christmas, we had all that we needed.

Some years, we'd do more than break even. We'd actually earn a profit, and we'd have a Christmas that fulfilled our expectations. Daddy would get a Christmas tree from the river's bank, and we'd place it in the living room and decorate it with homemade decorations using whatever we had available–candy canes, strings of popcorn, large red and green bulbs, and twinkling bright lights. We only had one string of lights, but we would stretch them until they covered the whole tree from top to bottom. We hung cotton on the branches to resemble snow and tie pieces of colorful fabric into bows on the branches. Sometimes, instead of a Christmas tree, we'd get a cotton stalk, which was no less beautiful than actual pine trees.

The seven of us never wrote out Christmas lists because our parents knew exactly what we needed–food, clothes, and shoes. Sometimes we'd get a small toy, but that was only when the bonus was bigger than what Daddy expected.

One Christmas, Daddy and Momma made a large profit, and we all got brand new coats! That year, everyone got something they really wanted. Momma took time to wrap each of our gifts. She didn't have nice wrapping papers, so she used newspapers and brown paper sacks. My brothers got a little red wagon and army men, cap pistols with matching holsters, and match box cars. My sisters and I got real rubber baby dolls with clothes and bottles to feed them and jack rocks and a ball.

On Christmas, I was always the first to go to sleep, afraid that if I was still awake by the time Santa Claus got to our house, he would put sand in my eyes. One Christmas, I went to sleep so early that I woke up in the middle of the night thinking that Christmas morning had come.

I slowly rolled over and peeked from under the cover, and to my surprise, Momma and Daddy were standing near our Christmas tree with a sack full of toys. Here, I was thinking that Santa Claus had been taking slugs of Momma's chocolate cake in the middle of the night, but it was Daddy all along.

Farm workers were hardworking and diligent, but they were still subjected to harsh and unjust treatment, especially when it came to being paid on time. Every time payroll came around, Mr. Bill would drag his feet, not paying his workers until Saturday evenings. Nevertheless, workers were still back on the field bright and early on Monday morning. Workers never dared to confront Mr. Bill for his treatment, but this is not to say they never found a way to even the score.

Everyone on the plantation which had a car was stealing gas from Mr. Bill, even Daddy. One morning as the men met at the shop to gather their tools for the day's work, Mr. Bill came speeding down the dusty, dirt road, as he usually did. The men watched as Mr. Bill's rickety, old pickup truck came flying toward them, stopping in front of the group of men that gathered at the shop. He walked up to Harper, one of the older workers who was sitting on a tractor tire and stood over him.

"Why ain't there no gas in that combiner there, Boy!" he yelled. His face was as red as a turnip. "Didn't you just fill that thang up yesterday?"

By that time, everyone had stopped what they were doing, waiting quietly to see how Harper was going to respond to Mr. Bill.

Harper stood up, "Well, sir," he began, "I, uh," he stumbled and fumbled over his words. "Yes, sir, I did–" he took a deep breath and began again. "Ay, you know, Boss? That gas just has a way of evaporating overnight."

Mr. Bill glared at Harper, but he didn't say anything. If his eyes were knives, they would have ripped Harper to shreds. Harper stared back, expressionless. Mr. Bill knew Harper had been stealing gas from the combiner at night to fill up the tank in his car, but he had no solid proof other than a half-filled tank on his combiner and tire tracks leading to the shed.

Finally, with one last glare, Mr. Bill turned around, walked back to his truck, hopped in, and sped away. As soon as Mr. Bill was out of sight, all of the men burst into laughter, including Harper. After all, they were all guilty of stealing Mr. Bill's gas to fill up their tanks.

Gas wasn't the only thing that the workers stole from Mr. Bill. Sometimes they'd steal Mr. Bill's soybeans to feed their hogs. Usually, hogs ate slop or leftovers from family meals, but leftovers were scarce if the family was too big. So, the second-best option to make sure that their hogs were well-fed was to steal soybeans.

One day, Mr. Bill noticed that the beans in the storage house looked a little slack. Mr. Bill's sifted through the large bins that the workers used to hold the soybeans after they were picked. After many days of harvesting, Mr. Bill expected a certain amount of beans to fill the storage house, but on this particular day, what the workers actually picked varied drastically from his expectations.

"Now, I know from all the soybeans that ya'll] harvested this week, it should be more beans in this storage house," he said to the workers, "and what I see right here ain't all the beans from that there field."

No one responded to Mr. Bill's accusations because everyone had been stealing Mr. Bill's soybeans. Everyone just watched Mr. Bill as if they had no idea what had been happening to the beans.

"These beans ain't vanishin' into thin air, I know that much," he continued. Sweat dripped from his pasty face that had begun to turn red.

Still, no one made a sound.

"Alright now," he said, "No one ain't gotta say nothin', but I sure will get to the bottom of it sooner or later. And when I do–," Mr. Bill said, squinting his eyes.

He didn't have to finish his threat to strike fear in the hearts of the workers. They knew what they had done but knew that Mr. Bill was capable of setting the record straight.

The workers didn't steal from Mr. Bill for fun. They stole to balance out whatever Mr. Bill had cheated them out of. Besides, if Mr. Bill insisted on cheating them, they had to find *some* way to provide for their families and make ends meet. I was too young to understand everything that happened, but I was smart enough to know that just like Mr. Bill was doing some underhanded and conniving things. The workers were simply returning the favor.

Even though the workers stole from Mr. Bill, he still found the need to give them all tanks of propane one winter. Propane tanks could be used for kitchen stoves, which made cooking easier and faster than cooking on a wood heater. Propane stoves made other everyday tasks like washing dishes and running bath water faster too.

Few people from the plantation had propane stoves, but fortunately, we did.

Mr. Bill was never the gift-giving type, so the only explanation behind him giving the workers propane tanks was to somehow get something in return later down the road. The workers were convinced that Mr. Bill only bought the tanks so that they would have to pay him every time they needed to fill it up. Mr. Bill soon learned that that idea wasn't going to work.

In our house, every time our tank got low, Daddy would fill it back up. For a while, I didn't know where he kept getting the propane from because it sure wasn't Mr. Bill, and I never saw a gas truck come to refill the tanks. When the tank was running low and the stove was on, the smell of propane would fill the house, which signaled Daddy to go get some more. I never saw Daddy buy any propane, but I also never missed a warm bath. Something just didn't add up.

One night, when I was sound asleep, I was suddenly awakened by what sounded like car tires rolling over gravel rocks. Our house sat right in the middle of the Gin Lott, and with all of the farm equipment surrounding us, including gas tanks filled with propane.

I creeped out of bed and tiptoed to the front of the house. It was dark outside, making it hard for me to see, but I could hear what sounded like Daddy huffing and puffing.

Normally, the dogs would go crazy if someone was lurking around our house, but they didn't make a sound. I looked a little harder into the nighttime darkness and noticed a figure slowly rolling a bottle of propane toward the house over the rocks in our front yard. I looked a little harder. It was Daddy! Daddy had been stealing Mr. Bill's propane.

Workers not only stole for themselves, but they stole to help others as well, especially single mothers. A few of the men on the plantation were dating some of the single women, and the women didn't have to worry about anything they needed.

The workers were masters of disguise. They all appeared to be so innocent and trustworthy, but Mr. Bill had to have seen straight through all of them. I always wondered if the reason why most of the workers never got out of debt was that Mr. Bill knew they were ripping him off.

There were several cafés and bars in Minter City where the men would go to eat and drink. On Saturday nights, the cafés made big money serving chicken and fish. Daddy loved going out to the small food and drink joints, but Momma wasn't the "hanging out" type. Momma called every joint Daddy visited a "hole in the wall." The only alcohol Momma ever drunk was Morgan Davis, and even that was consumed in extreme moderation. Daddy would buy her a bottle, and every so often. She would take a sip.

Daddy would hang out until late. Sometimes, it would be two o'clock in the morning before Daddy came walking through the door. Sometimes he would come home early with a greasy sack of fish or chicken.

When Daddy would stay out late, he would come home pretending that he was too drunk to get out of the car. He'd park the car right at the porch and slump over the steering wheel, resting his head on the horn, the headlights on his car shining through the window into our bedrooms.

When it came to drinking, Daddy was a lightweight, so it was always strange how he would manage to drive all the way home without ever having an accident. He never even did so much as ran into the porch. Either Daddy wasn't as much of a lightweight as we thought, or he was never drunk when he came home.

Momma saw right through Daddy's charade. She knew he was never as drunk as he attempted to convince her that he was. Daddy knew that Momma would be angry at him for coming home so late and spending money that he shouldn't have spent. So, to avoid Momma's scorn, he came up with the idea of acting drunk. Maybe then, instead of feeling Momma's wrath, he would get some of her sympathy.

Denise would always go outside and help Daddy into the house. He would pretend that he couldn't get out of the car and come into the house by himself. Sometimes, Denise would even lay in the bed with Momma to keep Daddy's spot on the bed warm until he got home.

Daddy played drunk so often that it became his Saturday night ritual. We'd gotten used to the headlights on Daddy's car glaring through our bedroom windows. We expected Daddy to come home late, park his car at the base of the porch, and wait until Denise came outside to help him into the house. But we never expected him to add to his act, until one night, he did.

One night, Daddy had been out drinking, and he let time catch up with him, as he always did. Daddy stayed out all night and came home at the crack of dawn Sunday morning. He staggered into the house like a sick patient.

Momma watched him as he walked through the living room toward the bedroom, but Daddy used all of his effort to not make eye contact with her. I could tell that Daddy didn't know how he was going to get out of the mess he had created this time. He was in hot water and had to think fast.

Daddy limped into the kitchen, grabbed the large tin can of flour from the cabinet, and walked to the back door. With one swift motion, he threw the whole can out the door. The flour danced in the air like falling snow.

Momma stood in the kitchen in shock. Her angry gaze turned into an expression of utter and complete confusion. We watched Daddy, startled at his behavior. After all, Daddy had done some crazy things to anger Momma, but we had never seen him do anything like this.

I believe Momma truly thought Daddy had lost his mind for a minute because there was no way possible that he could have been in his right mind for a second to throw out Ora Tanner's food.

Momma never said a word. She just stood and watched him.

Later that year, Daddy came home late after drinking, as usual. He tried the flour stunt again, but little did he know, Momma was ready for him.

Daddy came into the house and started toward the kitchen, but Momma stopped him in his tracks. She grabbed him by his shirt collar and pinned him on the wall.

"Now, Will, I got seven moufs to feed, and you know how hard it is to buy food for seven chill'en," she said, her lips tightly perched and her teeth clenched together. Her voice was low and calm. "If you ever even looked like you wanted to throw anymo' of our good food out that do', Imma kill you, you hear me?" She clenched Daddy's collar a little tighter. "That meal and flour cost too much for you to be chunkin' it out of the door." She let go of his collar and pointed her finger at him, less than a centimeter from his nose. "Long as you live here," she said," you bet' not ever throw scraps to the dog from my kitchen."

And as long as I can remember, Daddy never tried throwing flour out the back door again, no matter how drunk he got.

* * *

When we were younger, we couldn't wait for the fall of the year to come. We enjoyed the air's coolness, and we had waited for it all summer long. The fall weather was such a relief from the hot, blazing sun that we endured during the summer.

I loved the scent of cotton and the small particles of cotton dancing across the roads in the cool breeze. Hearing the sound of the cotton pickers and being out in the field, helping Momma pick cotton along with other families working was therapeutic to me. It was something about the sound of the farm equipment, the rumbling and loudness of all the different kind of machines operating at once that calmed me.

Everyone would join in picking the cotton that the machine left behind. They called it scrapping.

It was like a celebration for us every year, watching the workers pick cotton. We would count the times it took to go from one end of the field to the other. We watched how quickly the baskets that the workers carried would fill with cotton and how many baskets it would take to fill the trailer that waited at the end of the turn row. As soon as one trailer was filled with cotton, another one was pulled in place to be filled.

I can still hear the sound of the workers singing songs that only they knew, which helped them pass the time while working. Although the songs never made sense to me, I loved to hear the workers singing on one accord. Whenever one song ended, someone else would break out with another. The marathon of selections lasted all day long.

We enjoyed watching the leaves on the trees turn orange and brown, only to eventually fall to the ground, leaving lasting memories in my mind of the shade they provided in the summer heat. The huge pecan trees were loaded with pecans of all sizes. We would pick up every pecan we'd see. They were one of our favorite winter snacks to eat around the fireplace.

Harvesting time was one of the busiest times of the year. The men would work longer hours in order to get the crops in before it started raining and the weather dropped. Sometimes when it began raining, it would rain for days at a time.

For that reason, the workers would work late into the night to get as much done as they possibly could. The workers didn't mind working at night because it was much quieter and cooler, and Mr. Bill was not there to interrupt or slow them down.

During the beginning of the fall season, the workers enjoyed beginning each day bright and early. After working all summer in the scorching heat, they appreciated looking up into the blue sky and feeling a small gust of wind that chilled the air.

I can remember getting up early in the morning before leaving for school. I'd step out onto the front porch and gaze out across the fields. The vibrant golden sunrise slowly crept over the trees at the crack of dawn. The morning air would brush my skin and calmness would rush over me.

The mornings were always quiet and peaceful. We admired God's creations–the sights, the smells, the sounds all brought a sense of comfort to us. I loved listening to the chattering of the squirrels in the trees, chasing one another. I'd watch as the tall, half-naked cotton stalks rocked back and forth from the gentle breeze. The remnants from the cotton, beans, and wheat twirled along the road together in perfect harmony, racing one another to the other side of the road. The chirping of birds in the trees sang a soothing song, and the clouds moved across the sky in one calm motion.

In the evening, I would wait patiently to watch the sun fade away, gazing upon the beauty of its many glowing and different colors every day.

In no time, the trees were left naked with nothing to defend themselves against Old Man Winter. Birds began to take flight to keep warm and find food for the winter.

CHAPTER 12
MOMMA'S STORY

Momma was a short, dark-skinned, well-built woman with long, cold black hair. Momma always told us that she had Creole-Indian in her genes, but we never believed her. I think she just so happen to be a dark-skinned, black woman with long black hair that resembled that of the Creole Indians.

Momma was respected by everyone. She wasn't big on associating herself with a large host of friends, only socializing with a chosen few. For the most part, Momma stayed to herself.

Though she showed kindness and respect for everyone she came in contact with, you for sure didn't want to push her buttons; believe me when I tell you; she didn't mind letting you have it. Momma believed that since she showed so much respect to everyone around her, she deserved that same respect in return.

Momma could put up with a lot of things, but one thing she could not tolerate was lying. On Saturdays, Momma would play with us in the front yard, dancing and stamping her feet in the dust. We had a little red and white record player and about three or four records. We would dance until the sun went down, and Momma would be dancing right along with us.

Momma taught us to never depend on anyone for anything and instilled in us the idea that we could be whatever we wanted to be.

She was caring, sharing and loved her children, but she was very strict, especially on the girls.

Momma and Daddy would rise up early every morning, and the first thing we would smell was the aroma a fresh pot of coffee. Daddy was a real coffee drinker. He drank coffee every day of his life, making sure he got the pot rolling as soon as his feet hit the floor. After the coffee finished boiling, Daddy would wait for the floating grinds to settle in the bottom of the pot. The smell of coffee was our wake-up call to rise and get ready for another day.

By the time we got dressed, Momma would have breakfast prepared and waiting for us on the table before we were off to school.

There were times that Daddy only had time for his coffee because he had to leave so early. On those days, Denise, who had learned to drive a stick shift, would take Daddy his food before going to school. During the summer, one of us would have to walk to take Daddy his breakfast. Denise and Anita had to go to the field with Momma to work. Momma made sure that Daddy got his "sometee," as they called it back then. She gave us specific instructions for getting Daddy's food to him on time.

I remember Momma would never let us drink coffee.

"Coffee make kids hardheaded and disobedient," she'd tell us, but every so often, we would sneak a sip of Daddy's coffee. He didn't care if we had coffee or not. I never knew Momma's reasoning for not letting us drink coffee to be sound. I believe Momma was just trying to make the coffee last, and it wouldn't if she had to share it with seven other people.

We didn't always have a fancy breakfast. Most times, we just had biscuits, homemade syrup, and maybe a piece of salt pork or fried rabbit. It was rare that we ever got grits, eggs, or toast. It wasn't until we were a little older that Momma started buying oatmeal.

We never had a lot of any one kind of food, but for some reason, we always had rice. Momma made rice with every meal. When Daddy killed a hog, we would get fried country ham, rice, sugar syrup, and biscuits.

* * *

Momma would come home from the field tired and sometimes not feeling well, but she'd make sure that she made dinner for us. She'd come in and immediately start cooking supper. We'd eat, and then, Momma would heat water on that old wooden stove to give everyone a bath. Momma had a big tin tub that she would fill halfway with water to bathe the four smaller children. She'd bathe one after another in the same water.

Momma's work was never done. When she was done tending to us, Momma would wash all of our clothes by hand and hang them on the line. Load after load, Momma would rub the clothes on the washboard, sometimes until late into the night. When she finally would get her bath and lay down, she'd only have a couple of hours before it was time to get up and make breakfast, starting all over again.

She was strong and hardworking, repeating these chores day after day for many years. She only got a break when it rained, and she couldn't go to the field to work, but she still had many other chores around the house she would do. Even at the times when Momma was pregnant, she wouldn't stop working.

Women back in the day didn't stay home just because they were pregnant. They continued to work in the field all day long. Once it was time for Momma to give birth, she would have the baby, and in a few days, she was back in the field working again. There was no time for healing and bonding with the new baby; such was left up to the older siblings to do.

I remember hearing Momma moan and groan during labor. Then, after a couple of minutes, all that was heard was a baby crying. Momma's midwife would never let us near the room where Momma was. She only needed us to bring the water to the room. After we delivered the water to the door, she would tell us to go back outside to play. I always wanted to help, but the midwife kept us out. She was serious about her job.

* * *

When school was not in session during the summer, we all had to go to the field, even the smaller children. Too young to watch after the smaller children, Momma would pull the babies on the sack strapped to the front of her chest as she picked cotton, wrapping the baby tightly to her chest. Momma didn't like leaving us at home, so the only other option was having us all in the field.

I hated being out in the field with the hot sun bearing down on us all day long. The heat would drain and strip us of all the energy we had. When the evening approached and the dense shadow of the trees began to hang over and cover the workers, we knew that it was time to retire for the day. The sun going down was a great relief. We wanted nothing more than to clean our bodies from the sweat and dirt that had built up on our skin over the course of the day. After bathing and eating supper, we didn't have the strength to do anything more. So, we would all just go to bed. We knew that daybreak was coming soon, and we wanted to be well-rested before it did.

* * *

I'd help Momma can vegetables. From the vegetables in the garden, Momma made the most delicious homemade soups. She also made preserves and all types of jellies from apples, peaches, and pears.

Momma was a wonderful cook, and she was determined to teach me how to cook, especially her homemade biscuits. Of all the meals Momma taught me how to prepare, it took me the longest to learn how to make those biscuits. I'd watch Momma as she'd measure each and every ingredient, but when it was my turn to make them on my own, I never could get it right.

Momma whipped me many times for not making the biscuits correctly, but one day, I determined in my mind that I was going to learn how to make those biscuits if it killed me.

Before I began preparing to make the biscuits, I prayed and recited the list of ingredients in my head, over and over again. Then, I gathered everything I needed and began. It seemed as though the spirit of God was guiding me through preparation because for the first time ever, I made them just like Momma. It was one of the most joyous days of my life.

After years of working in the field, Momma decided that it was time for a change, so she applied for a job at the Baldwin Piano Factory. One day while working in the fields, she got a message that the piano factor had called the Slawson's store looking for Momma. She left the field to go to the store to call them back. When she called back, they called her in for an interview, and the following week, she got the job.

There were times that Momma had to catch a ride to work, but she got there every day. Momma was determined to keep her job at Baldwin no matter how she got to work. She had a hard time from week to week getting a ride all the way to Greenwood, but somehow, she always did it.

Momma worked at Baldwin for a long time, but eventually, she was laid off. However, momma had decided long ago that she was done working in the field. So, instead of returning to the plantation, she looked for other jobs.

When Momma heard that the Little Red Schoolhouse was in need of a helper, she applied for the position and got the job. She loved that job, and the staff loved her. Momma's job at the schoolhouse allowed her to bring more money into the house, which she used to buy groceries and get things we needed.

Daddy would take Momma back and forth to work. At first, he seemed happy about Momma's new job, but over time, I think he began getting jealous. For years, Daddy had been providing for the family, but with Momma's new position, she slowly became the breadwinner.

I think Daddy was also scared that he would lose her because she was dressing nicer, wearing her hair down more often, putting on lipstick, and she had her own money. Seeing how Momma was changing and fearing that one day, she'd up and leave, Daddy started to change too. He stopped going out and staying out late, and he seemed to start paying Momma more attention.

Even Momma's appearance began to change. She began buying herself fancy blouses, skirts, and slacks whenever she could. Working in the field, Momma didn't have the money or the reason to buy nice clothes but working in the schoolhouse changed both of those things.

We were happy to see Momma finally working a job that she enjoyed, no longer having to slave away in the hot sun.

We weren't rich, but we no longer had to worry about what we were going to eat or if we'd have clothes and shoes for school. Momma's job at the schoolhouse lifted all of our burdens, including Daddy's.

By that time, a new landowner had come and taken over the plantation. His name was Mr. Mark. Mr. Mark was much kinder and more caring than Mr. Bill had been. He wasn't demanding and was less strict on the women and younger workers.

Times were changing, and thankfully, they were changing for the better.

CHAPTER 13

UNCLE WILBER AND AUNT ROSETTA

Uncle Wilber and Aunt Rosetta lived beside us in the Gin Lott. Uncle Wilber had a large and stocky body. At six feet tall, he towered over us like a large oak tree. His hair was peppered, and his large teeth stacked on top of one another like blocks. His nose was large and round, the thick bridge of it dividing his two crossed eyes. If not for his tendency to point, we might never have known who he was speaking to.

He was married for some years to Aunt Rosetta. He was an old, evil man and treated her very unkindly. Sometimes he would jump on Aunt Rosetta and blacken her eyes for no reason.

We all loved Aunt Rosetta. She was one of the kindest people in the world. You'd never see her without a smile on her face, but after the long conversations talking to Momma, we soon came to realize that Aunt Rosetta was miserable living with Uncle Wilber. After years of putting up with Uncle Wilber's abuse, Aunt Rosetta finally got tired and decided that she'd had enough. She made up her mind that she was going to leave him and go live with her sister in Louisiana.

Aunt Rosetta told Momma of her plan to leave, and Momma told Daddy. Daddy wasn't a man of many words, so he didn't really say much about it. I think deep down; he didn't want Aunt Rosetta to leave our uncle since they had been together for a very long time. But, Daddy knew how hateful and abusive Uncle Wilber was.

Aunt Rosetta gradually packed her belongings over the course of months, hiding them at our house. Every few days, Aunt Rosetta would wait until Uncle Wilber left for work and call Denise to pick up boxes to take them to the mailman to be shipped off. Denise would stand watch, looking out for Uncle Wilber to make sure he didn't come back to the house in the middle of them moving the boxes out of the house. For months, Denise helped Aunt Rosetta mail off boxes until she got all of her things shipped to her sister without ever tipping off Uncle Wilber that she was planning to leave him.

After Aunt Rosetta left, Uncle Wilber never married again. After all, there was probably no one left in the world that would've wanted him.

Uncle Wilber and Aunt Rosetta's house was the most popular house in the Gin Lott. Their house operated both as a residence and a store. They sold everything–cookies, candy, gum, sodas, chips, every snack a kid could want.

In addition to helping Aunt Rosetta operate the store, Uncle Son worked on the plantation. He drove the tractor and operated other farm equipment. During harvesting time, he worked at the gin separating seeds from the cotton in preparation for the cotton to be processed.

Uncle Wilber worked at the gin for many years until one day when he was working, his legs accidentally got caught in the machine. Before anyone was able to stop the machine, both of his legs were broken. Since Aunt Rosetta was long gone, our family was the only people available to help him through his difficult time.

Even though he was a mean old man, we still loved and cared for him and hated seeing him in so much pain. So, we did all that we could to help him get back on his feet as soon as possible.

He had to use crutches for months, and when he no longer needed crutches, he still had to walk with a cane for the rest of his life. After the accident, Uncle Wilber walked slower, and he'd developed a limp as he shuffled around, leaning on his sturdy cane to distribute the weight of his body.

He didn't only use his cane as an artificial leg, but when he would get angry at us, he'd lift it from the ground and swing it at us. Sometimes, he would even take his cane and try to hook it around our leg to pull us closer to him so that he'd have a better shot at hitting or pinching us. He'd always make sure Momma was nowhere to be found before he proceeded to terrorize us.

"Now, if he do anything to any of ya, let me know," Momma would tell us, and she'd make sure to solve the problem. Momma didn't trust Uncle Wilber for a minute because she knew how mean and hateful he was.

Uncle Wilber would come to the house and sit with us on the front porch every night. And every night, we'd try to get rid of him to no avail. We'd hate to see him coming because we knew that he wouldn't want to go home when he came.

"Be nice, and if he asks you to do something, gone on and help him out," Momma warned us just before Uncle Wilber would get to the front step.

When he came with a sack of snacks, we'd easily be nice. But when he came empty-handed, all bets were off. Momma didn't like for him to bring us snacks because she would say he was trying to bribe us. He'd usually bring us goodies when he knew that Momma was upset with him.

He didn't like for Momma to treat him coldly. She wouldn't laugh and talk with him, and she'd all but ignore that he was even present. For some reason, this always got under Uncle Wilber's skin. He wanted to keep her happy.

Uncle Wilber knew Momma didn't care for his ways–how he treated others, how rude he'd be– but she would still do whatever she could for him.

He was needy and demanding, always wanting us to do him favors. If we hesitated or didn't want to comply with his orders, he would get angry and tell Momma we'd been mean toward him or that we were being disobedient, any lie he could think of.

Uncle Wilber was a great liar, so great that they would sound like the truth. Momma would fuss at us and even whip us about things Uncle Wilber would tell her, and she wouldn't give us the chance to defend ourselves. He was like a hawk, watching us, trying to see what we were doing.

He would sit with his hands propped under his jaws, pretending to be asleep. All along, he would be watching our every move, looking for trouble so he could tell on us. There was never a time when Uncle Wilber would just come and visit with us without starting trouble.

None of us could stand Uncle Wilber, but I put up with him more than my other siblings. After all, I loved to eat, and Uncle Wilber knew he could always win me over with a sack full of cookies and candy. Anita despised our uncle, and for him, the feelings were mutual. He never liked her because she had a smart mouth and always talked back to him. They were like oil and water.

Over time, uncle Wilber and I started getting along very well. Our bond had grown, and I became one of his best friends. Denise and I were the only two that he got along with because we'd do a lot for him. We'd go and clean up his house and wash clothes for him. I would cook him food and wait on him hand and foot. Any way I could, I helped him. I felt sorry for Uncle Wilber. He didn't have anyone close to him to help take care of him, and as his health was failing.

He trusted Denise so much that he even gave her a key to his house. When the delivery man would come to bring Uncle Wilber's packages, Denise would be there to accept the delivery when Uncle Wilber wasn't home.

If Denise wasn't working in the field with Momma, he would allow her to run the store. She'd come home with so much stuff that she'd have to hide everything so that Momma wouldn't find it. It wasn't often that he let her work in the store, but whenever he did, she brought home enough snacks to open up her own store.

We ate for days, and our younger siblings didn't have a clue of where all the snacks were coming from. They just ate along with us. We never told Momma or Daddy, and our uncle never seemed to have missed anything from his store. The younger siblings were too young to remember to tell Momma about what goodies we had given them. When Momma and Daddy would leave for work, Denise would get the stash of looted snacks, and we'd have a field day. Denise would hide the snacks so well that no one would have ever known her stash even existed. I never even saw Denise's stash.

When Denise finally left home, our uncle began clinging to me more. I would continue to help take care of him, and he would give me change for my troubles.

After he had gotten hurt at the gin, he became a slob, not bathing or changing his clothes for days at a time, and when he would eat, he wouldn't even bother wiping his mouth or his hands. Uncle Wilber had a habit of rubbing his hands together and then rubbing them through his nappy, yellowish hair. Boy, that would send chills up Momma's spine. Momma would fuss at him for his sloppiness, but her fussing did nothing but offended him, causing him to stay away for days.

When Uncle Wilber got sick or hurt, he stayed with us until he was nursed back to health, even when he got hurt at the gin. When he stayed at our house, Momma made sure he took a bath and cleaned himself. She always had to fuss at him, but she took good care of him in time of need.

When he got hurt at the gin, Mr. Joe, another plantation owner, hired a nurse to come help us out with him. The nurse would come at least three times a week. As he started getting better, the frequency of her visits became less regular.

A few years later, he became Mr. Joe's wife's personal driver. Anywhere she needed to go, he would take her.

Once Uncle Wilber couldn't work in the fields anymore, he began working inside Mr. Joe's house doing light chores like letting the dogs out or taking out the trash and cleaning the silver and China.

Momma would sometimes tease him by telling him he was Mr. Joe's bus boy.

Mr. Joe had a large dog named Bruin. He'd growl and bark at everyone who passed, but to be honest, he was just as scared of us as we were of him. Still, Bruin kept us afraid of him for so many years. Whenever Uncle Wilber was at Mr. Joe's house, he never made Bruin behave. He knew how afraid we were of Bruin, but it amused him to see us running from him carrying big buckets of water, spilling the water as we clamored to get away.

We told Momma about how Uncle Wilber wouldn't control Bruin when we passed by, and she sure did get onto him about it.

"Now, if that dog bite one of dem chill'en, you gone be in a world'a trouble," she said.

Whenever we went to the well to get our drinking water, Bruin would always chase us. We had to pass Mr. Joe's house to get to the well, and Bruin would be camped out, waiting on us to come near. When we'd come back from the well, our buckets would be with water.

The minute we heard or saw Bruin coming, we'd take off running and waste most of our water. When we got home with buckets only half-filled with water, Momma would make us go right back to the well to get more. Sometimes she would come meet us and make Bruin go back into the yard, but we never had the guts to do anything except run.

One day when Momma asked me to go get water from the well, I decided in my mind that I had enough of Bruin. I was tired of running, and I wasn't going to run anymore. I made up my mind that when that dog came after me, I was going to fight back. Just the thought of standing up to Bruin made me sick, but I had to do what needed to be done.

I picked up my bucket and a big stick and headed for the well. On the way to the well, I was shaking in my boots, walking slowly and keeping an eye out for Bruin. I stepped over leaves and maneuvered around sticks that would serve as sirens, alerting Bruin that someone was on their way to get water from the well. Even though I couldn't see him, I knew he'd be coming sooner or later.

When I finally made it to the well, a wave of relief swept over me, but it was short lived. Out of nowhere came Bruin, charging at me, what seemed like the speed of light.

I sat my bucket down on the ground and looked Bruin right in the eyes. My body was trembling all over and my heart pounded as if it were trying to escape from my chest, but I didn't move. I stood in that spot, stick at hand, and watched as Bruin ran toward me.

Now was the time to show Bruin who was boss. Like a raging bull, I took off toward Bruin, determined to show him that I wasn't taking any more of his mess. When that dog saw me running toward him with my large stick, he began to slow down. Finally, he came to a complete stop, turned around, and began running back to toward the house. Boy, I must have struck the fear of the Lord in old Bruin because after that day, he never felt the need to chase us from the well. Every time we'd go to the well, Bruin would just lay in the yard and watch us go by.

CHAPTER 14

HENRY JONES

Henry was our step-grandad. He was married to our grandmother for many years, and they had two children together. Momma was the oldest of all her siblings. She helped her mom in caring for the younger children.

Henry was a clean-cut, well-dressed man with a petite figure. He kept himself groomed and only wore clothes and shoes of the finest quality. His hair was white as snow.

By the time I was old enough to know him, Grandma had long left him. After all, he wasn't the easiest man to get along with. He was cheap and stingy and didn't like sharing anything.

He loved smoking. Everywhere he went, he carried his long pipe, and he could often be seen with it hanging out of the corner of his mouth with smoke shooting out of it like a freight train.

Now, Henry was meaner than Uncle Wilber. None of us really cared for him. We tolerated him just because he would always come to our house with our uncle. And just as much as we couldn't stand them, they couldn't stand one another.

Momma never liked Henry because she knew how terrible and hateful he was after growing up in the same house with him. According to her, she left home at an early age to keep from killing him.

As years went by and Henry's health began to fail him, he longed for Momma's company more and more. Even though he knew Momma didn't care to be around him, he was at our house every chance he got. When Momma would cook, he was always there begging for whatever was left over. There weren't anything left over most times, not even a crumb, but he would still wait around to see if there was *something* he could get. When Momma would cook vegetables, Henry called the juice from the vegetables "pot liquor." When there were no vegetables left over for Henry to have, he would just drink the juice.

Henry always seemed to have something ugly to say. When Momma decided to give him something to eat, he would act nice appreciative in receiving it. He would sit on the front porch quietly and eat whatever food Momma had given him, but once he finished eating, he would get up slowly and walk out into our yard, throwing the dish back onto the porch. As soon as he would get to the road, far enough away from our house, he'd call out to Momma, telling her that her food was nasty and unseasoned. Momma would get so angry and throw things at him, but he would run into his house, jumping and laughing.

Sometimes when he would eat dinner with us, he'd snatch food from our plates. Without notice, he'd walk up to us and take our food, then laugh in our faces.

"Now you betta leave my kids alone," Momma would warn him, but that never stopped him from coming back the next night and doing the same thing.

Momma would tell Daddy to get a hold on Henry before she had to, but it seemed as though the more our parents got on to him, the worse he would act. When Daddy would get on \him, he'd get so offended that he'd stay away for weeks. Then, he'd start coming back around again and be up to the same antics.

Storms scared Henry. If it rained or thundered too hard, he wou-ld come over to our house and bang on the doors and windows, begging Daddy to let him in. If Daddy was upset with him, he would leave Henry out on the front porch through a few loud claps of thunder and bright bolts of lightning. Daddy would be tickled watching Henry from the window, trembling and steadily banging on the door.

"Lemme in, Will! I promise I ain'tgon' act ugly no mo'," he'd howl above the wind, but we all knew that his promises were the furthest things from the truth.

Daddy would finally let him in, and we'd all sit around the living room, riding the storm out together. As soon as the storm was over, Henry would leave, and on his way out the door, he'd be back to his usual self, hurling insults and laughing about how he made a fool of my Daddy. Daddy would just tell him to go.

Henry and Uncle Wilber would come to our house every night and sit on the garret with us.

One night when we were sitting out on the porch, enjoying the nice evening breeze blowing through the trees, they came over. There were lighting bugs flying around, crickets chirping, frogs croaking, and dogs barking. It was a perfect summer night to be sitting out on the porch, but the tension between Uncle Wilber and Henry sure knew how to make even the most relaxing night stressful.

Daddy and Momma sat on the front porch while we played in the front yard. The night was still and peaceful, interrupted only by Uncle Wilber and Henry's arguing over who wore the best clothes.

"I jus' bought these bad new boots and a lumber jacket. Boy, I tell ya! I'm not gon' be able to keep the ladies off me," Henry said.

"You can't dress," Henry objected. "That's why none of the women don't want nothin' to do with you now." He stamped his feet in amusement. "Ya clothes always nasty, and the moths seem to get to 'em before you do," Henry continued.

Uncle Wilber watched Henry angrily as his insults kept coming.

Finally, Henry stood up, walked out into the yard, and began dancing. He twisted and turned and clapped his hands to imaginary music.

"I know you wish you could move like this, huh?" he asked, closing his eyes as if he were getting lost in the music.

Uncle Wilber sat forward, leaning his weight on his cane. "I don't wish nothin', and that ain't no dancin'. You so thin that if someone fried all the grease from your body, it wouldn't be enough oil to dot the letter 'i'," Uncle Wilber said, and this time, we all joined in his laughter.

That was enough to push Henry right to the edge. Henry ran over to the edge of the porch where Uncle Wilber was sitting smoking a cigarette, his cane on the ground beside him, and all of a sudden, Henry drew back his arm and slapped Uncle Wilber right upside his head.

Unfortunately, Uncle Wilber thought faster than Henry could run. He picked up the cast iron skillet that was sitting on the porch, and before Henry could run far enough away, Uncle Wilber launched that skillet directly at Henry, hitting him square in his back. Henry let out a screech and fell to his knees, his pipe still hanging out the side of his mouth.

In amazement at what had just transpired, we all gazed upon Henry's limp body lying in the yard. For a minute, we thought he was dead. After a couple of minutes, Henry jumped up and began walking back to the house. He appeared to be in a daze, not knowing what had just happened.

Finally, Daddy ran over to see if he was okay. He grabbed Henry around his waist to help him regain his balance, and Henry flung his arm around Daddy's shoulder.

He looked at Daddy, then back at the porch full of spectators and began to laugh.

"That didn't even hurt," he said, "but I will get you back for that, Wilber. You better watch your back."

Daddy helped him take his seat back on the front porch, but after a few minutes, without any warning, he stood up and walked home.

We thought Henry would settle down after getting hit that hard, but he didn't. He started carrying his gun down in his boot everywhere he went, and every time he'd come around Uncle Wilber, the playful banter that once happened between them turned into purely hateful insults.

Chapter 15
BESSIE "HOOGER" JONES

Our grandmother was Bessie Thomas, but we called her Hooger. She was married to Henry.

Hooger was a tall, slim gray-headed woman. She worked hard and was very devoted to her family. She also helped raise many of her grandchildren, including the seven of us. She always had a positive message to share, and she treated everyone with kindness.

Just like Momma, Hooger didn't mind coming off the porch to play with us and enjoy our company, but still, we always kept a certain level of respect for her because she didn't mind reminding us that she was still our granny.

Hooger and Henry lived right beside Mr. William's house. With Henry working for Mr. Joe, another landowner. Hooger worked for Mrs. Betty, Mr. William's wife. She cooked and cleaned, and Mrs. Betty treated her well. Hooger liked making her own money, considering she couldn't depend on Henry for anything. For as long as I can remember, Henry never supported Hooger. He was a terrible person and an even worse husband.

As a child, Hooger would come spend nights at our house often, but I didn't understand why. We would love for her to come and stay with us for a while. She'd help Momma cook and make beautiful quilts and flannel gowns to sleep in during the winter. At night, she'd tell us bedtime stories.

It wasn't until I was older that I realized why Hooger stayed with us every so often—to get away from Henry.

If Henry wasn't blackening her eyes, he'd be threatening to do it. He'd sleep around with other women and stay out late. Hooger would get tired of dealing with his abuse and infidelity, so she'd come stay with us.

When Hooger would stay with us, she came with rules that we didn't usually have to follow. Her first rule was that we had to get along. She didn't want to see us fighting or bickering. She made sure that we were being nice and respectful to one another, so we'd just end up sneaking to hit each other or make snide remarks. She would also make us wash out our socks and underwear and hang them by the fireplace to dry at night. Each of us only had a couple of sets, so she wanted to make sure we had clean under wear for school every day.

The seven of us knew not to question anything Hooger told us to do. We followed her rules without question or hesitation. We loved her visits, but after a while, we'd be happy to see her go.

* * *

After enduring Henry's mistreatment for so long, Hooger couldn't bear putting up with Henry any longer. So, she decided that she was going to move out. She and Henry separated, and Hooger moved to Greenwood to be closer to her two other daughters and her other grandchildren. She only came back to Sunnyside to visit us.

CHAPTER 16

THE STORY OF DENISE

Duenise was always a sweet, obedient, and respectful young woman who always tried her hardest to please Momma and Daddy. Though she respected them both, Denise was a Daddy's girl, and in his eyes, she could do no wrong. Every day, Denise would bring Daddy food to the field where he worked, no matter how far away the field was. She'd walk to bring his food up until the point she was allowed to drive. Daddy took Denise everywhere with him, but their favorite activity to do together was to go fishing on the McIntyre Lake near Money, Mississippi.

Her calm and peaceful spirit and her desire to help others made her loved by everyone.

I thought she was so pretty and had a body that was out of sight, she had a nice figure and her clothes fitted her really well.

When Denise was old enough to begin working in the field, she became momma's right hand. She'd go to work with Momma in the field during the day; then at night, she'd come home and help Momma with all of the chores. She'd help Momma cook, bathe my younger siblings, and stay up until late at night to help Momma wash and hang the clothes. Momma had a special relationship with each of her children, but there was something about Denise that made her and Momma's bond tight.

Denise was the perfect big sister. She cared for us and got along with us well. She never scolded us or whipped us when we did anything wrong, but with her nurturing spirit, she corrected us with love.

* * *

For school, Momma packed all of our lunches, and we all had the same exact meal, even Denise, who was in junior high. Momma would pack the same meal every day—rabbit and biscuits or salt pork and biscuits wrapped in newspaper and placed in a brown paper sack.

Denise would be embarrassed because once you became a teenager, you became too cool to carry a paper sack lunch. Children whose families were better off dressed well, and they always had lunch money and ate in the cafeteria and those who didn't tried their hardest to convince their peers that their family was well off too.

Denise wanted so badly to convince her peers that her family had money. She dressed well for the most part, thanks to our aunts from Missouri who'd occasionally send us clothes and shoes, but sometimes, she was forced to wear a pair of black kitten heels with socks that belonged to Momma. Those heels were the only nice shoes she had to wear, but to wear them with socks was beyond embarrassing. Sometimes, she would get dressed slowly to miss the bus so that she wouldn't have to go to school. She couldn't stand wearing those heels and socks to school.

"Now, I'm tellin' ya now, gyal, if you miss that bus, I swea," Momma would threaten, leaving Denise to run after the bus in those kitten heels and socks.

She'd run past the men who were working on the road, seething with anger. When she got to school, she'd roll down the socks to make them look better, but that didn't help. Nothing could make that combination look any better.

It was hard for her to truly sell her "rich girl" act wearing those heels and socks in addition to never having enough money to buy even a three-cent carton of milk.

Thankfully, she was not alone in her struggle. She had a friend named Sharon, who was also poor but did everything she could to convince her peers otherwise. On the days Denise and Sharon had brown sack lunches, they'd eat their lunch together in the shed behind the school instead of the cafeteria.

When Momma started getting commodities from the government, Denise was a little less hesitant about taking a brown sack lunch. The rest of us were actually excited to bring lunch to school. With commodities, low-income families were given free groceries, boxes filled with crackers, cheese, bread, and jelly. Momma would pack our lunches and we'd be ecstatic to see a peanut butter and jelly sandwich instead of salt pork between a biscuit.

That commodities program had some of the best cheese and lunch meat that anyone could ever want. With a lunch meat sandwich and a three-cent milk, it was easier for Denise to appear as though her family was doing well. So, when the commodities program began,

Denise and Sharon began eating lunch in the cafeteria with the other children whose families were well off, or at least who appeared to be.

Eventually, Denise began eating lunch in the cafeteria even more often when she started working for a white family that lived on Sunnyside Road on the weekends and sometimes on the weekdays after school.

* * *

The only time Denise and I would argue was when she'd ask me to fix her ponytail. Her hair was short and rather difficult to manage, but she insisted on attempting to wear a bang and a ponytail every day. Every morning, she'd come to me with a string and a comb for me to help her tie her hair up, and every morning, I couldn't. I tried as hard as I could, but her hair was too short to make the string stay. She'd snatch the string away as if it were my fault and be off to do it herself.

Even though Denise was the oldest, she still played with the rest of us. During the winter, the garden down from our house would freeze over, and we'd pretend it was an ice-skating rink. We called it the "truck patch," and children from everywhere would come to the rink. One day, while playing in the truck patch, Denise fell face-first on the ice. Immediately, her nose began to swell. She didn't seriously hurt herself, but the embarrassment that she felt was painful enough. From that day forward, the other children gave her the nickname "Ice."

* * *

Denise was in charge of the house when Momma and Daddy weren't home. One day, Momma instructed Denise to smother some chicken, cook pinto beans, and bake some cornbread for dinner while she was out. Momma gave Denise specific instructions on how to prepare the chicken, and it was already cleaned and ready to be cooked.

When Momma came home, the smell of dinner danced in the air. Momma started making plates for the younger children, but she soon came to realize that the chicken was not on the stove. She called Denise into the kitchen and looked at her. Denise was smiling deviously.

"Denise, where's the chicken?" Momma asked.

"Behind the bed," Denise answered, her smile beginning to break.

Momma gazed at Denise. Anger and confusion filled her face. "What do you mean behind the bed?"

By this time, Denise was no longer smiling. Her brown eyes swelled in her head, and she began to fidget nervously. "Yes ma'am," she said. "You told me to smother it. So, I wrapped it in a towel and put it behind the bed."

Momma's face flushed with anger. We didn't have any food to be wasting on childish pranks. What Momma didn't understand was that Denise honestly didn't know what she meant about smothering the chicken.

Momma grabbed Denise and turned her every way but loose! Daddy tried desperately to pull Momma off Denise and stop her from whipping her, but it was nothing he could do.

Denise learned that day how to smother a chicken. She never had problems cooking anything else.

* * *

Denise was naturally nervous and shy, but that didn't stop her from dating. The first guy she dated seriously was Bob. He was a school bus driver. Back then, if young guys who were in school had a drivers' license, they'd be paid to drive the school buses. Denise met Bob at T.Y Fleming High School, and since they were dating, she became the queen of the bus Bob drove. No other girl was allowed to sit on the front seat behind the driver because that seat was reserved for Denise.

Other girls took a liking to Bob too, but none of them stood a chance against Denise. They'd talk about Denise among themselves, but it didn't matter because Bob only had eyes for her.

Denise always took a special concern for how she looked. She never went out of the house without looking presentable. She wore nice pleated skirts and flowy blouses, and when Bob planned on coming over, she spent hours getting ready, curling her hair and finding the perfect outfit.

The first time Bob ever came over, Denise cleaned the house from top to bottom, hoping that while Bob visited, the rats would not also choose to make an appearance. When Bob arrived, he knocked on the front door lightly, and Denise rushed to open it. He stood on the front porch, smiling nervously. After a minute, Daddy came to the front door and invited him inside. The rest of us peaked from the back room to see what was going on.

Denise took him into the living room, and they sat down to talk. They had not been sitting for very long before some unwanted visitors found their way out of the loft and into the living room. Denise tried to keep her composure while trying to see where the rats were coming from and in what direction they were going. She looked toward the kitchen, and low and behold; several huge rats were gathered on top of the stove, themselves to some crumbs from the biscuits that were leftover from supper.

She turned around to Bob, her face flushed with embarrassment. She thought for sure that he had seen the rats and that he would never want to come visit her again, but he didn't say anything about them.

After that first visit, Bob began coming over more regularly, and he and Denise started going steady.

Bob, like most young guys, didn't have their own cars. In order to go see their girlfriends, they had to carpool. On any given evening, you could see a car full of boys driving down the dusty road, each one getting dropped off at their girl's house. The carpool system was pretty effective, but the only problem was that sometimes, the driver didn't do pickups, only drop-offs.

One evening, Bob's ride dropped him off late, but it never came back to pick him up. That evening, Bob ended up having to spend the night with us, sharing the bed with Daddy. He later told Denise how miserable and afraid he was. Apparently, he didn't get a wink of sleep because he was too afraid of accidentally touching Daddy.

After two years of dating Bob, they got married, and she left home. Denise leaving hurt as much as death, but I never told her how much it bothered me. I didn't want her to worry about me, even though she probably wouldn't have anyway. Denise wanted to explore the world. To see what else was out there for her other than the cotton fields. I believe the only thing that may have bothered Denise for a moment was leaving our Daddy.

I knew how tired Denise was of living in Sunnyside and working in the fields, and by marrying Bob, she was finally free.

CHAPTER 17

THE STORY OF ANITA

Anita was the most fearless of the bunch. She was courageous and determined and always found a way to get what she wanted. She was enthusiastic and headstrong, which often could be mistaken for hardheadedness. She was hard working and didn't mind getting her hands dirty working in the fields.

Anita was the second oldest, so she was second in command to Denise. If Denise was not around, Anita was in charge. When Momma and Daddy would go to Greenwood on the weekend, Denise and Anita were responsible for us.

On Saturday nights, most parents would go out, so young guys used Saturday nights as their chance to go see their sweethearts. Sometimes, we'd see figures walking around the house or see faces peeking through our windows through the thin curtains. Sometimes we'd hear sounds of someone creeping in the yard or scratching on the windows. Denise would be scared, but Anita was never afraid.

We had two old dogs named Whitey and Brownie. They were the sorriest guard dogs anyone could ever have. They wouldn't bite anything but a biscuit. As soon as it got dark, they would start barking and growling uncontrollably, but they soon would bring all the barking to a halt, meaning whoever they were barking at was someone they knew well.

Daddy had a rack of all kinds of guns he kept hanging on the wall. When we'd hear people outside, Anita would tell us to turn out the lights and she'd grab one of Daddy's guns. Our front door was old, and it barely held on by the hinges. It had a hole in it just big enough for the barrel of a shot gun to fit in.

Anita would put that gun through the door hole and fire it a couple of times without giving any warning. When the ringing in our ears died down, we could hear those young guys running as if Anita had been shooting at their feet. Anita would let off a couple of rounds, and soon enough, the figures that were lurking around the house would be gone.

The guys who'd come lurking around our house wanted nothing more than to come and talk to Denise and Anita, but as long as Anita was around, that that didn't happen.

* * *

Growing up, everyone had certain chores to do around the house. One of Anita's chores was feeding the hogs. Anita hated those hogs. So, every chance she got to feed them, she used it as a chance to hurt them.

Anita dealt with feeding the hogs for so long that one day, she got so aggravated with them climbing over one another to eat that she just snapped. After trying to put the hog's food in the trough but not being able to because they kept rushing her, Anita had had enough. She put down the slop bucket and started walking toward the house with a sort of determination in her step.

She looked around near the porch, grabbed a garden hoe, and then started back toward the hog pen. Every time a hog would jump up when she tried to feed them, she'd whack it with a hoe. She kept whacking until her anger built up into a frenzy. All of a sudden, she was just whacking them all. I ran out to the pen and grabbed her, begging for her to stop, but it was too late. The hogs squealed in terror and blood stained their coats.

I couldn't wait for Momma to come home so that I could tell her what Anita had done to those hogs. I knew for sure that Anita was going to get a whipping so bad that she wouldn't be able to stand it. If Momma got to her before Daddy, she would have really hurt Anita. But Anita was smart. She knew that Momma would be the first to come home, so she left just before Momma got there. She ran into the woods to wait for Daddy to come home.

When I saw Momma coming, I took off running too. I couldn't wait to tell her how Anita had cut up our hogs.

"Momma, you won't believe what Anita did to our hogs," I said, trying to catch my breath.

I told Momma how Anita used the hoe to slash the hogs and how she ran into the woods just before she got there. Momma was so furious that she went looking for Anita in the woods, but she couldn't find her. When Daddy got home and found out what Anita had done, he immediately got in the car and went looking for her. It was good and dark by the time Daddy found Anita.

He brought her back home, and Momma was still angry. Daddy wouldn't let Momma whip Anita because he knew that if Momma got hold of her, she'd put a real hurting on her.

Daddy was always protective of Anita because when she was younger, she fell out of the car as he was driving. He always blamed himself and never forgave himself for Anita falling out of the car.

For months, Daddy had to doctor the hogs to get them back healthy, and the chore of feeding them was taken from Anita and given to my brothers and me.

* * *

Anita was rather mischievous. She always found trouble to get into. When she would stay home with us while Momma, Daddy, and Denise worked in the fields, she sucked us into her mischief.

She's make us steal watermelons and cantaloupes from our neighbors' truck patches by threatening to put snakes or worms on us if we didn't listen to her and do what she said.

Our neighbor, Mr. Otis, was the easiest victim. He knew that we were stealing his melons, so one day, he told our dad that he would put poison on them that would make whoever stole his melons never stop laughing. Daddy came home and told us what Mr. Otis said, not knowing that we were the ones who were stealing his melons.

"I guess we ain't gone never stop laughing," Anita whispered.

Though Anita bullied us into being mischievous, no one else could bully us as long as Anita was around. Anita loved fighting, sometimes fighting just for the fun of it.

One time, while hanging out under the large persimmon tree with our friends, Anita and her friend Dora got into an argument that escalated into a physical fight rather quickly. Denise tried to break up the fight, but Anita would not let up.

Denise spent a lot of time trying to protect Anita and keep her out of trouble, but to no avail.

One cold day, Anita was coming home from working in the field. Even though she had on layers of clothes, she had to come into the house to get warm. When she backed up to the fireplace, she got too close to the fire and immediately, her dress tail caught on fire.

Momma immediately grabbed a bucket of water and dashed it on Anita. She put out the fire but the steam made her burns worse. We all watched in horror as Momma wrestled Anita to the ground to try to get control of the flames. Her skin seemed to be melting off her body like hot lava.

When Momma and Hooger, our grandma, finally got the flames and Anita under control, they brought her into the house and laid her on the bed. She was burned so badly we thought that she wouldn't make it through the night.

Shortly after, Daddy had gotten the news and rushed home. He had been out in the field working. Daddy and Momma rushed Anita to Greenwood Leflore Hospital.

The Slawson's allowed our parents to give the Hospital their phone number in order to contact them concerning Anita's condition, and they always made sure to get the message from the hospital to our parents. We were afraid to see them coming at times out of fear that they would tell us Anita's condition had gotten worse.

For several years Anita was in and out of the hospital. She had to get several surgeries, and Momma had to spend many days and nights at the hospital with Anita.

Our Aunt Lizzie didn't live too far from the hospital, so she made sure to go check on Anita every chance she got. Some days, she'd go to the hospital to relieve Momma of her visit so that Momma could go home and get some rest. Aunt Lizzie was always sweet to us; she bought clothes and food for us many times.

I remember Momma would send Denise to Greenwood with one of our neighbors. Aunt Lizzie would go to the grocery store across the street from her house and buy momma all kinds of food to send back by Denise. It was nothing she wouldn't do for our Momma.

Denise also spent countless nights with Anita to relieve our mom. The rest of us were too young to stay at the hospital with Anita.

The first time Anita came home from the hospital, we were so happy to see her. Whatever she wanted or needed one of us to do, we were always right there. She couldn't walk for some time. For a while, she had to slide around on her hands and bottom. She went back to school for a little while, but it was too difficult for her to maneuver. I tried to help her as much as I could by helping her get on and off the school bus and carrying her books for her, but Daddy saw how tough it was for her to keep attending school, so he decided to just make her stay home.

Though Anita never seemed to be bothered by her predicament, seeing her like that bothered me. What bothered me even more was seeing other children laugh and tease Anita.

Anita's final surgery was on her legs. She had physical therapy for some months, but soon enough, she was able to walk again without the help of crutches.

Eventually, Anita decided that she wanted to go back to working in the fields again. She worked according to her ability and strength.

As time went by, she told Momma that she wanted a real job. She believed that she could handle factory work. Sometime later, she applied to work at Baldwin Piano Factory and she got the job.

With her new job at the factory, Anita began helping my parents out more, buying groceries and paying bills. One Easter, she bought all of us new Easter clothes and shoes. She bought dresses and frilly socks for the girls, and nice suits and dress shoes for the boys. Anita bought our first sofa. It was a red-orange love seat. We loved that little sofa. Later on, we were blessed with a stereo system with a lift top and storage on each end. It was about six feet long and the music played so clearly. We would play our forty-fives records for hours as we danced around on the porch.

Anita had been through a lot throughout her life, but she never quit, and with determination and the help of God, she made the best out of her situation.

When Anita finally left Sunnyside, she moved to Chicago and got married to her long time friend. Without Denise and Anita at home, the responsibilities of tending to the younger children and keeping up with household chores in my parents' absence fell on me.

Chapter 18

THE STORY OF ORA

As a child, I enjoyed playing in the playhouse that I and my sisters built out of pieces of tin, wood, and bricks. It had tin walls and wood flooring. We stacked bricks to build a stove and used buckets for tables and chairs. We'd pretend that the playhouse was an actual house, cooking and serving dinner, cleaning, and inviting guests over for dinner parties. We pretended to cook large meals for our husbands and children. Woodchips were pretended meat, and grass was greens. Dirt and water made delightful pretend hoecakes. We used old cans and lids from jars as our dishes.

Our baby dolls were homemade from soda pop bottles and old rags. We'd wrap old rags around the bottles and use whatever else we could find to add to them. Sometimes, we would sneak in the garden and pull off the young ears of corn from the stalk to play with as our baby dolls. The corn would just be at the beginning stage of producing the young corn. It had long yellow silks shooting from the top of the corn stalks, which we pretended was our babies' hair. We would comb it for days until we combed it bald. We'd have corn everywhere, and it wasn't long before Momma realized what we were doing and put a stop to it.

"We don't got food for y'all to be wasting," she said, "I bet' not catch none of ya in that garden again."

Growing up, I was always the one to tell Momma or Daddy when one of my siblings was doing things they had no business doing. My intentions were never to get anyone in trouble, though I could never convince them otherwise, but to keep them from hurting themselves. Walter hated me for that. Walter and Anita were always the ones being reported, but that was because they were always the ones being mischievous.

I was a sickly child, always contracting fevers or strep throat. Momma would do all that she could to doctor me back to health. She'd only take me to the doctor if I got so sick that she couldn't help me anymore.

Most people couldn't afford going to the doctor, so they made home remedies to cure common sicknesses. Momma would make us wear muster plaster to fight off the flu or a cold. She'd hold it over the fire to get it nice and warm; then she would pin the cloth to our night gown or under shirt in order to keep it in place over our chest area. Sometimes the muster plaster would cause our skin to blister if applied directly to it. Momma would put the muster plaster on our chest and tell us to go straight to bed.

Sometimes, Momma would wrap a dirty sock around my neck to cure my strep throat. I wanted to believe that putting a dirty sock around my neck really cured me, but I know it didn't. Every hour,

Momma would ask me if I was feeling better. I'd get tired of her asking me the same question over and over, so after a while, I would lie, telling her that I felt better.

When I wasn't battling a sickness, I was playing with my siblings. There was a hill near our house that we'd play on whenever it rained. We would take turns sliding down the hill in the gumbo mud that covered it. One time while sliding down the hill, I decided that I would be creative and slide down backwards.

As I slid down the hill, I felt something hit the back of my heel. As soon as I got to the bottom of the hill, I looked at my heel, and, to my surprise, blood was covering my foot. I looked around to see what had caused my injury and noticed a thick piece of glass from an old coke bottle protruding from the hill. It sliced my heel open at least two inches deep.

When I noticed the skin of my heel hanging open, I began to scream. Everyone stopped and watched. **Denise** came over, picked me up, and walked me home.

When Momma saw what had happened, she didn't get hysterical or even scared. She simply got a a pan of cold water and began putting pressure on my open heel to stop the bleeding. She used a piece of fat meat and sulfur to pack the opening of my heel and tied up the wound with a rag. I had to stay off my feet for a few days, and within a week, I was fine. I never got a fever or an infection and never even took any medicine other than aspirin. Amazingly, the wound didn't even leave a scar.

* * *

I always tried to help Momma and Daddy with whatever they had to do. Sometimes, I'd try to surprise them, but more often than not, my surprise backfired. One day, I decided to cut the weeds and clean up the garden for Momma while she was at work so that she wouldn't have to do it when she got home. I spent all evening tending to that garden, but when Momma came home and looked at the work I had done, she was less than happy.

"Gyal, you cut down all my vegetables! Who told you to go out there and chop that garden?" she asked.

I shook my head, afraid of what Momma was going to do to me. Fortunately, she recognized my good intentions instead of my poor execution, and she let me go with no repercussions.

One summer, I decided that I would clean up the yard and clear out all the dead weeds and grass. I wanted our yard to look beautiful, so I started a fire to burn all of the weeds and grass that covered the yard. I raked the grass and weeds in one large pile, and as soon as I struck the match, it seemed as though the entire yard was set ablaze. Momma saw the flame and with swiftness, got a bucket of water and threw it on the flame. A few buckets later, the flame was under control. This time, she wasn't so understanding. Momma whipped me so terribly that I never wanted to go out into the yard again.

* * *

Daddy would always ask me to get up no matter what time of day or night it was to make him what he called a hoe cake of flour bread and some onion gravy. Not once did I ever refuse to do what I was asked, even though sometimes I really didn't feel up to it, but my parents never knew. Once I got in the kitchen and began making that hoe cake of bread and gravy, the aroma from that onion gravy just pierced the air.

When I was a teenager, Momma would pretend to be sick. She'd complain that she had a headache or that her blood pressure was up. Oddly enough, she'd always be sick on the weekends. On Saturday and Sunday morning, she'd call me into her room and ask me to make breakfast explaining that she couldn't because of how horrible she felt. Weekend after weekend, I got up to make breakfast, but I knew that Momma wasn't really sick. She was just tired of having to get up on Saturdays. For years, I let Momma act out her sicknesses until one morning I had had enough.

I marched into Momma's room and stood over her bed. She had the most pitiful look on her face.

"Listen Momma," I said, "I know you not sick, and you never were. I don't mind helping out around here, but you can't keep faking." I felt good for finally standing up to Momma.

Momma looked up at me, wiping the pitiful look off her face, and she burst into laughter. "I was wondering when you'd finally catch on," she said, wiping the tears from her eyes, unable to contain her amusement.

Helping out around the house and being on my best behavior did nothing to get me the perks of being the oldest child in the house. Whenever I wanted to go to ball games or parties, it would take me a week to build up the nerve to ask Momma if I could go, and the answer was always "no." I heard the word "no" so much that I began to think my name was No.

Every weekend I looked forward to the next time to ask my Momma if I could go out, prayerful that one day she'd say "yes" but prepared to hear another "no." There were times I wanted to go out and have fun so bad; I would actually go to sleep and dream about it.

In my dream, I would be out kicking up my heels, dancing and having a good time, only to wake up in my bed.

When I went to school on Monday, everyone would be talking about where they went and what they had done for the weekend. I would lie to my friends, pretending that I went to a dance or to a game, but honestly, I had nothing to share. I talked a good game and acted like I had it going on, but the truth was Momma wouldn't let me go anywhere, being so strict and overprotective. It seemed as though Momma was stricter on me than she'd been with Denise and Anita.

The only places I could go to were school, the corner store, church, and my part-time job on Saturday mornings. I worked for a police officer that lived on the Sunnyside Road past the schoolhouse. Momma liked us working. She didn't mind me making a little extra money to buy things I needed for school. I would work three to four hours a weekend for fifteen dollars. That was good money back then. Every week, I'd save up my money to go shopping in Greenwood on the weekend.

In addition to not being able to go anywhere, Momma also didn't like me dating. Whenever Momma was around, boys on the plantation wouldn't dare to even come near. They'd just walk by, look, and smile because they knew they were never going to approach Momma to ask her permission to date me.

Most of my socializing were done at school. Sometimes the school would host a social. A social was a dance during school hours. Since I couldn't go to parties after school, I made sure that I went to every social that was thrown. I would prepare for the upcoming social from when I got home from school until I left for school the next morning. When the time came for the social to begin, I was the first one there, ready to hit the dance floor, dancing up a storm to every song that was played. I knew it would be a while before I got another chance to party with my friends.

During the month of May, the school would host what we called "May Day." May Day was a day set aside to celebrate the end of the school year. There would be food, games, and music. Sometimes parents came to support and partake in the activities. My favorite activity was "platting the May pole," where people would tie long, colorful strings of ribbons or crepe paper around a tall pole. Platting the May pole was the high light of the May Day festival.

When school let out for the summer, we could hardly wait to get back to school in August. Everyone would be so happy to see one another to show off their new clothes and shoes. We all had stories to tell about what we did or where we went during our summer break. When it all boiled down, most of us hadn't done any more than we did every summer, which was working in the field.

However, once Denise and Anita left home, they would send for me to come to Chicago for the summer. I would babysit for them while they worked. While staying in Chicago, they'd buy my clothes, accessories, and shoes for school. After all, they were once teenagers, so they knew how important it was to come back to school with nice clothes, and after years of wearing those flour sack print dresses, I was ready for a change.

Although I loved visiting Chicago and enjoyed my summers there, I would always be ready to come home.

The new school year didn't only introduce new clothes and shoes but also new skin tones. Everyone would come back to school shades darker as a result of working in the fields all summer long. By the fall, every ones' skin would be back to its original shade. In high school, some of the girls discovered a cream called "Ultra Bleach and Glow." Most of them only used it on their face and neck area but forgot to put it on their arms and dark legs. They would come back to school looking like white girls in the face but black girls from the neck down.

Their faces lightened and became smoother, but the rest of their bodies went unchanged. I saw what the cream did for others, and I wanted to try it out, but Momma wouldn't let me. I had sensitive skin issues.

Even though I didn't take part in everything that my peers did, I never had a problem with making and keeping friends. Debra and Freda were my best friends since middle school. We were always together, and we shared like sisters. We shared everything from jewelry and clothes to paper and pencils.

We even shared the struggle. One day, none of us had lunch money, so we decided to go to Mrs. Franklin's house. She was one of our schoolteachers, and she lived right beside the school. We were embarrassed to have to ask one of our teachers for food, but we had no other option. We were starving that day. Mrs. Franklin made each of us a sandwich, gave us a carton of chocolate milk, and sent us back to school.

We saw some rough days. On more days than I can remember, we didn't have lunch or lunch money. We'd find nickels and pennies on the ground, and as soon as we had enough money, we'd sneak out of the school building to the store across the street and buy snacks. If we were caught, we would have been in big trouble.

Ms. Martha, the store owner, always welcomed us with a kind smile, and she always gave us more than what we actually could afford.

* * *

In middle school, I won homecoming queen, and Debra and Freda were right by my side. On the day of the homecoming game, they helped me get dressed to make my homecoming queen debut. I wore a long white gown with elbow-length white gloves and a crown on my head. In the fall of the same year, I won homecoming queen again when I went to high school. Being crowned homecoming queen twice in one year was one of the most joyous memories of my life.

Debra and I lived within walking distance of each other. We rode the same school bus and played together every day. We always had a good time together, always laughing. Sometimes we'd laugh so much that the bus driver would threaten to kick us off the bus.

I met Ellen in high school, and we became fast friends. Over time, she became more like a sister to me. We were together so often that people began to think we resembled each other. We were like Bonnie and Clyde, partners in crime, known for getting into trouble together.

Ellen knew how to sew, and she'd make us matching outfits. People would be waiting on us to come to school just to see what outfits Ellen had whipped us up over the weekend.

Her father lived up north in the city, and he would send her an allowance every month, which she always shared with me. Whatever she bought for herself, she bought me.

* * *

I met Aaron in third grade, and we kept in touch all of our life. We would write love notes and letters to each other and ask mutual friends to relay them between us. Whenever I missed school, Aaron would always send me a love letter by my brother Walter.

"Do you like me? Check 'Yes' or 'No,'" the letters read.

At school, we walked and held hands, and he would carry my books to the school bus every day. We hated to say goodbye at the end of the school day because it always seemed like tomorrow took forever to come.

Growing up, Aaron was shy. When we were face to face, he hardly ever had anything to say. He'd just smile and watch me, but by the end of the school day, he would always build up the nerve to kiss me on the cheek as I boarded the bus to go home.

For a while, we could only interact with one another at school. Aaron never asked me to come visit him at home. Momma never liked the idea of us entertaining young men, but Daddy never had much to say about it.

On a day Momma was leaving to go visit Denise and Anita in Chicago, Aaron decided to show up at my house unannounced and unexpectedly. He stood on our old, broke down porch, waiting at the front door. I could see his big, brown eyes piercing through the door. He had a wide grin on his face. When I looked out and saw Aaron standing on my porch, my heart began to pound. I was scared to death.

Daddy went to the door and invited him into the house.

"Hello, Mr. Tanner. Is Ora home?" I heard him ask. I watched him from the other room, scared to death of what Momma was going to say when she came from her room with her luggage, preparing to leave.

After a few minutes, I came into the living room and sat on the sofa. Momma was still in the back, getting ready to leave for the bus station. Finally, she came out of the room.

Momma glanced at Aaron, then at me and back at Aaron. "Well, hello," she said, a confused look covered her face. "How you doing?"

"Hello, Mrs. Tanner," Aaron responded nervously, "I'm fine."

Momma paused for a second, then she continued, "I'm sure you came here to visit Ora, but I'm about to leave for Chicago, so you're going to have to leave. But, you're welcome to come back to see her on another day when I get back," Momma said politely.

My heart skipped another beat as it danced for joy inside of my chest. Momma's invitation for Aaron to come back let me know that I was now of age to receive company.

Aaron stood up, looking confused. "Yes ma'am," he said.

Momma left to finish what she was doing in the other room, and Aaron headed toward the door. However, as soon as Momma left the room, he turned around and gave me a kiss on the cheek. As he stepped onto the porch, he turned and looked back at me for a moment with a smile, seemingly attempting to hide his disappoi-ntment.

I was happy that Aaron stopped by, but I felt bad for him because whoever had dropped him off was now long gone. He had a long walk home, and the absence of streetlights and the light from the moon, that walk was a little longer.

Aaron and I kept in touch throughout the years, and eventually, we got married.

CHAPTER 19

THE STORY OF WALTER

Walter was the fourth child and the oldest boy. Growing up, we all called him Man.

Walter was petite in stature and had smooth brown skin. We teased him incessantly about his large nose, and he'd get so angry to the point of wanting to fight. Walter always had an impish look about him, leaving us to wonder what mischief he was planning to get into.

Walter had a mind of his own, and in every situation that he was subjected to, it was his way or no way. He also had a habit of doing just the opposite of what he was told to do. Momma whipped him regularly, but even switches demand Walter's obedience.

As a young child, Walter thought that he was supposed to accompany Momma and Daddy everywhere they went. Every time they would leave, Walter would throw a fit in protest of them not inviting him. One day, when Momma and Daddy were leaving, Walter threw the biggest tantrum that he'd ever thrown. My sister held him in her arms, attempting to calm him down, but he flailed like a fish out of water. After a few minutes of trying to restrain him, he finally broke a loose and begin running alongside the car. Momma told Daddy to stop the car. She was fed up with Walter acting a fool, and this would be the last time he did so. She got out of the car and broke a switch from one of the trees that line the road to our house. She came around the car, grabbed Walter, and whipped him with the power of God.

That whipping changed Walter's life. After that day, he never ran after the car again. When Momma and Daddy would leave, he'd just sit on the front porch, crying and pouting but never daring to get off the porch to chase the car.

Though Walter always got into trouble, he was smart and hard-working. He never had a problem doing chores, and when he was older, he began working in the field to bring in extra money.

Walter was the first of the five younger siblings to get a real job outside of farming. His first job was in Greenwood. He worked for a factory called Picture Frame. The factory made all kinds of picture frames and shipped them all over the world.

Since Walter was the next oldest, he sometimes thought I was his younger sibling. Though Momma and Daddy left me in charge in their absence, Walter never liked for anyone to have control over him, including me.

One day while Momma, Denise, and Anita were out working in the field, Walter decided to go out in the garden, even after Momma specifically told us to stay away from her garden. He sneaked out through the back door and ran into the garden. He crawled on his stomach like a snake, moving through the rows of crops. I begged him to come out of the garden, but he refused.

"You're going to break Momma's vegetable plants," I called out to him, but he continued crawling.

After a while, I grew annoyed, so I grabbed the first thing I could find–a Mister Cola bottle. The bottle was a large, thick glass soda bottle that we used to hold water. I was tired of calling and pleading for Walter to come out, so I waited, watching the bushes move to track his movements. When I finally got a good glimpse of where he was going, I raised that bottle in the air and threw it at him, hitting him square in his head. He fell out like a cockroach that had been sprayed with Raid.

I stood still, waiting for him to jump up laughing like he would normally do, but this time, he didn't. He was out cold for a few minutes. I ran out into the garden calling him, but he didn't answer me. When I finally found him among the vegetables, I looked at the top of his head and it was rising like a cone. The swelling began immediately.

I began to panic.

I slid my arms under his shoulders and dragged him to the house. I began putting cold rags on his face and head.

He finally started to wake up. "What's going on? What are you doing?" he asked, still dazed and confused.

"I'm trying to save you," I answered, ringing out another towel over a tin bucket.

I nursed him for a few more minutes, and soon, he was back to being himself. I'd never been so happy to see Walter being himself.

Walter never told Momma what happened, maybe because he didn't want to get both of us in trouble, me for throwing a bottle at his head and him for playing in Momma's garden or maybe because he didn't actually remember what happened. Either way, I never got in trouble for what I had done, and Momma never seemed to notice the knot on Walter's head. After all, I made sure to do all that I could to make the swelling go down.

As children, Walter and I got many whippings for fighting, but the whippings never stopped us from fighting. The last fight that we had growing up was a Friday afternoon. It had been raining sporadically throughout the day. While playing outside in the rain, Walter and I started arguing.

At first, we just traded insults, but when Walter spat on me, it was on. I grabbed him by his collar and hit him across the head. We traded slaps, kicks, and jabs for so long that we both grew tired. I used every ounce of strength I had to hit Walter and defend myself against his licks. He was hitting me so hard that I wonder whether he knew that I was a girl.

All the while, Momma sat on the porch in her rocking chair as if she didn't even notice us fighting. She didn't say anything or even attempt to try to stop us. She just rocked back and forth, waiting for us to tire ourselves out.

Finally, when we stopped fighting, Momma called us to the porch. She had in her hand what appeared to be a tree, but it was only a couple of twigs tied together. Momma whipped both of us terribly, and from that day forward, Walter and I never fought again.

* * *

Walter always had a love for swimming. He always wanted to swim in the Tallahatchie River behind our house. He was fascinated by the water but I was terrified of him getting in the river because he was so small, and the snakes and sinkholes made the river very dangerous. But none of that fazed Walter.

Jim was one of Walter's closest friends. He was a white boy whose family had a farm a few miles away from where we lived. Momma, Denise, and Anita would work on Jim's family's farm picking cucumbers sometimes.

Jim would walk for miles just to come to our house to play with Walter. They would sit around outside in the yard shooting marbles or just talking. Honestly, Jim was too old to be hanging with Walter, but of course, we couldn't make Walter see that. Jim was a little slow, so guys his age probably didn't play with him as much as he'd have liked, but Walter didn't mind.

Walter and Jim would play around until they thought no one was paying attention to them, and as soon as they thought no one was watching, they would sneak off down the hill toward the Tallahatchie River.

I told Momma that Jim and Walter had been sneaking off to swim in the river, but I had no proof to convince her. Until one day, when they decided to take a swim, I followed them. I watched in wait for them to take off their clothes. They took off every piece of clothing they had, hung it on a limb, and jumped into the water.

This was my chance.

I ran up to the limb, collected all of their clothing, and then darted back up the hill to the house. As soon as I made it halfway up the hill, Jim and Walter emerged from the river. They saw me running away with their clothes and yelled for me to bring them back, but I kept running. Jim cursed at me to bring his clothes back while Walter yelled to leave Jim's clothes and only take his. I considered bringing

Jim's clothes back, but I quickly changed my mind because I need all of the proof I could get.

I wasn't trying to be a snitch, but with so many kids drowning, I didn't want Walter to be one of them.

I tried to keep Walter safe as best as I could, but with Walter, there was only so much I could do. Walter had gotten a safety pin stuck in his nose. Momma and Daddy were gone, and I was left in charge. He was so hysterical that I couldn't figure out what to do. Blood streamed down his face and stained his clothes, and his large nose was swelling. I ran him over to Mr. Tommy, a tractor driver who was still at the shop across from our house preparing to start work for the day.

"Come here, boy," Mr. Tommy said, reaching for his toolbox and pulling out a pair of needle-nose pliers. He stuck the pliers in Walter's nose and pulled out the pin. Walter howled like the man had shot him. "Now take him back to the house and put some cold water on his nose. He gone' be alright," Mr. Tommy said, sending us away.

Unlike the bottle incident, we couldn't hide this incident from Momma because Walter's nose stayed swollen for a few days.

* * *

As Walter got older, his whole demeanor changed. He became interested in political and public matters. He wanted to know how the governmental system worked and what rights we had as American citizens. Walter had always viewed life through a len of curiosity and wonder, always challenging the norm and living according to his own set of rules.

CHAPTER 20

THE STORY OF MARGIE

My sister Margie was the fifth born. Margie was quiet growing up. She never liked getting into trouble. We would pick on her just because she wouldn't fight back. She was afraid of getting whippings. She didn't talk much when she was younger. As she got older, she became more talkative, and after a while, it became hard to shut her up.

She had a nice body build and long legs, so whatever she wore made her look like a model. The only physical aspect of Margie that we could tease her about was her large feet. By twelve years old, Margie was already wearing a size ten.

Growing up, Margie had to sleep with me at times. She was always lazy about getting up to go to the potty. So, she would just lay in bed and wet herself on purpose. I would be so angry at her; I would put her out without any covers.

Margie loved to sleep, but when Momma asked us to get up and clean the house, Margie would spring out of that bed like a rooster.

Margie enjoyed playing alone. She didn't really care for having friends over. The most she needed was her siblings, but she was just as much at peace playing by herself. After all, she had many imaginary friends, which she considered to be as real as could be.

As time passed, Margie slowly began coming out of her shell. She became more active and wanted to engage more with others.

Margie was our comedian. She was always joking and doing funny things, keeping us laughing. Margie thought everything was funny, which wasn't always the case, and many times, her sense of humor would get us in hot water.

She was fun and humorous, but she also had a dark side. She could always do something she had no business doing but still manage to convince Momma that someone else did it. We loved Margie for her storytelling, but it all depended on the story.

* * *

One of Margie's favorite meals was syrup and hoe cakes. She could really put away some syrup and bread. She'd sop up the syrup so fast that it barely even had time to stain her plate. When we ran out of bread, Momma would hide the syrup to keep Margie from drinking it.

Margie was our granny's favorite granddaughter. She always wanted Margie to come and stay with her. Even when Margie would be mischievous, Hooger would intervene on her behalf, stopping her from getting into trouble.

When Hooger left Sunnyside and moved to Greenwood, she still allowed Margie to come stay with her for weeks at a time during school breaks. She'd sneak and buy Margie toys and snacks and try to hide them from her.

Margie loved sweets. Once, when she was about nine years old, Margie had a craving for something sweet. She found a week-old newspaper and took it to the boss's wife's house. She planned to trade the newspaper for a slice of cake. When the boss saw the date on the newspaper, he came and told momma what Margie had done. When Margie saw the boss coming, she darted ran down the hill to the riverbank.

Momma called for Margie to come out, but she knew she was in big trouble. When Momma finally got hold of Margie, she whipped her like she had stolen a herd of cows.

When Margie became a teen, she had many friends. People liked her because she knew how to have fun and keep you laughing. Margie was the life of the party.

"When y'all get off that school bus, change ya'll clothes and come straight on to the field." Momma would tell us.

We'd all be rushing to get out of our school clothes to get to the field, but Margie would just linger around taking her time. She never really liked working in the field. I would fuss at her and try to make her hurry up because I knew that Momma would be waiting and watching for us. If my brothers and sisters didn't get to the field fast enough, I would be held responsible.

Margie was never a dancer. When we would dance in the front yard for hours, she would just sit and watch.

When Margie got older, she began working in Greenwood at a senior citizen facility called the Care Inn. She was always quick to catch on to anything.

How have you learned to care for the patients so well? You never had training," I'd ask Margie.

"Well, the proof is in the pudding." She'd say, "A person can learn to do whatever they want to."

"I wouldn't want you caring for me," I'd tease.

Chapter 21

THE STORY OF BETTINA

Bettina was the youngest girl, and we spoiled her rotten. As a little girl, she was very active, getting into whatever she could get her hands on. Bettina always loved dancing and pretty clothes. She was a great dancer and an even better dresser. She would do anything to keep her image, whether it meant borrowing, begging, lying or, stealing. She always had a smart mouth and learned to talk back at an early age. She would talk back to anyone because the last word always belonged to Bettina. Whippings didn't faze her one bit. She would talk back and fight whoever was up for the challenge.

When Bettina was about two years old, Momma had washed clothes one night, as she would do many times during the week. This particular night, Momma didn't empty the tub of water, so it was left until the next day. Before Momma left for work that morning, she told us to make sure we emptied the tub of water when we got up. As the day moved along, no one had taken out the tub of water.

Throughout the day, Bettina would run by the water and splash in it. Bettina had been running around all day, but at one point, we realized we hadn't seen her running around. We looked for her throughout the house and soon found her face down in the tub of water. We drag her small, limp body out of the water while shaking and pressing on her chest. She had begun turning purple, and she was not breathing. After a few minutes of attempting to resuscitate her, she started crying and kicking. The fear that we had of losing our sister was all that we needed to save her life.

For the rest of the day, we kept a close eye on her and waited on her hand and foot.

Bettina got into trouble more than she stayed out of it. In middle school, Bettina was chosen as the class treasurer. At one point, she had about forty dollars of the class's money in her possession. Rather than keeping it somewhere safe, Bettina decided to spend every dime of the class's money. When the time came that the class needed the money, Bettina didn't have it. Instead of admitting what she had done, Bettina went to Mr. Felix, the store owner, and asked him to borrow forty dollars, which she said was for Daddy. When Daddy found out what Bettina had done, he had to pay Mr. Felix back little by little. Back then, forty dollars was a lot of money to borrow from someone.

Bettina had a bad habit of borrowing money and getting things on credit in Daddy's name. She would tell Mr. Slawson that Daddy said to let her borrow five or ten dollars. Then, she would go up the highway to another store and tell the owner of that store that Daddy said to let her get some gas on credit.

All of the store owners knew our parents and had faith that they would pay them back for whatever Bettina got, but Daddy wouldn't have a clue that Bettina was borrowing money and getting stuff on credit until after Bettina had already been there.

Daddy and Momma got tired of bailing Bettina out of trouble, especially when she got in fights at school. I remember the last time Momma went to Bettina's school and had a talk with the Principal.

"I'm not making no more trips up to this school," Momma told Bettina's principal, "I'm done with this child and her foolishness. Do whatever you want with her."

Momma and Bettina's principal were ready to write her off, but she always had a way of getting people back on her side. She always managed to convince her principal to let her back in school.

In high school, Bettina's behavior hadn't changed much. Bettina would get into a fight almost every day. She got put out of school almost as much as she went to school. If she wasn't fighting in school, she was skipping school. She would board the school bus at home, and when the bus got to Greenwood, she would get off at the railroad track. A lot of kids would get dropped off at the track to skip school and spend the day in Greenwood, and since all the bus drivers were teenagers, they could care less about letting the students off the bus.

* * *

Bettina eventually finished high school, by the grace of God, and she started working. She wanted to work and support herself, but if she felt overworked and underpaid, she would quit a job in a heartbeat and have another one in days.

Though Bettina stirred up a lot of mischiefs, she was a people-person. No one was a stranger to her. She could entertain anyone, anywhere. She could walk in a room, and in minutes, everyone in the place would be gathered around her, laughing and talking with her. She had a way of capturing the attention of people wherever she went. She had a great personality and knew everyone.

Some people, however, hated Bettina. She was attractive and social, and many of her friends were jealous of her, which is why she often got into fights.

CHAPTER 22

THE STORY OF ROGER

Roger was the youngest of the bunch. When he was first born, he had an olive color, and his hair was cold and black, laying close to his head. He had beautiful brownish eyes.

I claimed Roger at birth. I took care of him from the time he was born. He was always considered my baby, and he gravitated to me as if I were his mother. He wanted me to do everything for him. He didn't want anyone else fixing his food, giving him a bath, or even taking him to the potty. He would pitch a fit if anyone even tried to help him.

I had to take care of Roger. After giving birth to seven child-ren, Momma didn't mind letting me raise Roger. She needed a break.

It was something about Roger that made me fall in love with him from the time I first laid eyes on him. As a baby, Roger was a joy since he was so easy going, and he loved to cuddle. We all loved, pampered and spoiled Roger to the core.

Although Roger was the baby, he had chores just like everyone else. Particularly, Daddy would make him pick up wood chips for the fireplace and the stove. Daddy made sure Roger picked up enough chips every day to last us through the night. Roger was also in charge of making sure Daddy's trotline always had bait on it. Daddy would leave his fishing line in the water at the riverbank, and Roger was tasked with the chore of checking the fishing lines regularly. Additionally, Roger had to gather the eggs from the chicken coup, which Momma would use to cook with.

When Roger got a little older, he would occasionally go to work in the field. He'd carry water across the field to the workers and pack the cotton in the trailers as the cotton pickers dumped their baskets of cotton after filling their sacks. He always liked making his own money. To get paid on Saturday made him feel like a big boy.

Like Walter, Roger thought he was supposed to accompany Momma and Daddy wherever they went. Whenever they would leave, Roger would throw a fit. We had to hold him down until they were out of sight. He'd chase the car and wail in agony when he'd see Momma and Daddy driving away.

Daddy always had guns around the house. He taught Walter and Roger how to use them when they were very young, and he would let them watch him adjust and clean the guns. Roger became fascinated by Daddy's guns.

Anytime Daddy sat down to clean and adjust his guns, Roger was right there to witness it. When Roger got older, he seemed to think that getting a gun was the answer to all of his problems. Every time one of our siblings made him angry, to the gun rack he would go. We started to call Roger "The little Shotgun Shooter."

I hated that Daddy had taught Roger and Walter about using weapons. So, I sat Roger down and explained to him what could happen if he were to use a gun when he didn't need to. After our talk, he stopped going for the gun every time he got mad, but he would fight at the drop of a hat, regardless of how small he was compared to his opponent. When Walter and Roger got their first bike, they had to share it. Some days they played well together, but sometimes, they would fight over whose turn it was to ride. Roger was small but he always managed to stand his ground against Walter.

It seemed that we were to blame for many of Roger's actions beca-use we would let him have his way with everything. Momma never treated Roger differently; however, she whipped him just like she whipped the rest of us. We would take up for Roger and lie for him to keep Momma from whipping him. Sometimes it worked, and sometimes it didn't. Most of the time, Roger got whippings just like the rest of us.

In our family, my sisters and I knew that Momma loved us, but we also knew that she would kill for Walter and Roger. Momma didn't want anyone saying anything about those boys, whether they were right or wrong. No matter what, Momma defended those boys.

CHAPTER 23

THE STORY OF THE BRICK HOUSE

The first real home we ever lived in was a brick house. Our brick house was the first brick house ever built for blacks in Sunnyside.

After my sisters left home, they would write to Momma, promising to send money to help us with what we needed, and even though it took longer than they planned, they stuck to their word. They made sure we had clothes and shoes for school and money for groceries.

Daddy and Momma had grown tired of working on the plantation, and we'd all grown tired of living in the same old rundown house. It was time for a change.

Walter always had his ear to the streets, listening out for any chance to change our situation. Somehow, Walter heard about a bill that the government passed that would provide landowners with funds to build new homes for people who lived and worked on the plantations.

Walter was knowledgeable about political and social matters, so he told Daddy what was being said, and Daddy took Walter on his word. Most of the landowners had been keeping quiet about the funds, not wanting the poor black people to find out.

Later that week, Daddy went to speak to Mr. Bill, but Daddy was smart. He never mentioned that he knew about the government funding. Instead, he told Mr. Bill that he was just about out of debt and was thinking about moving. He explained to Mr. Bill that he was tired of living in such poor conditions. Mr. Bill knew that Daddy was one of his best workers, and he didn't want to lose him. So, he told Daddy to just hold on for a little while that things were going to get better.

A year later in 1966, Mr. Bill decided to have a meeting with all of the tractor drivers. He made a promise to the workers that he was going to build all of them a new house, but he never told them about the government funding. Everyone waited patiently for the rest of the year for their new home, but the building process didn't start until 1967.

During the summer of 1967, builders began breaking ground with the building of the first brick house in Sunnyside owned by the black people. Everyone waited in excitement and suspense because no one knew what tractor driver would get the first house. After they built the first brick home, they stopped building. All the tractor drivers waited on the rest of the homes to be built, but they never were. The tractor drivers were upset, but they never went to Mr. Bill to inquire about his promise to build them all new homes. Most people just assumed that he ran out of money. Some assumed that he just decided to not build anymore. Whatever Mr. Bill's reason was for not coming through on his promise was irrelevant. All that mattered was people who were promised a new house from Mr. Bill never got one.

* * *

After a year of building, Mr. Bill informed Daddy that the brick house would belong to us. Daddy and Momma told us to keep our mouths closed and to not tell anyone about the house. We had to wait until we knew that the information Daddy had received was true.

When Daddy finally confirmed the truthfulness of the information, all we talked about was the new house. This was the first time we were going to experience living in a nice home, and no one on the plantation had ever experienced having running water, central heating and air, and an inside bathroom. Our new home would have all of those things.

We had to pass by the building site on our way home, so we watched as additions were made to the home every day. When the builders first laid the cement, we'd sneak onto the worksite and stood on the slab. We witnessed them lay the foundation, then put up the frame then make a place for the doors and windows. Though the house was only in the beginning stages of being built, it was a beautiful sight to see.

As we anticipated the move, we were overwhelmed to move from the Gin Lott's shed and shop area to the black top road. We would no longer have to walk through mud and water to get home, but we had lived in the Gin Lott for so long, it was hard to believe that the Lord was ready to bring us out.

The brick house was built in a perfect location, right at the curve of the road facing the fields of cotton and beans.

There were nights that we hardly slept. We'd just lay in our beds talking about our new home as we eagerly awaited our move-in date. We could hardly wait for daylight to appear so we could go view the house again.

The house was made of red brick and had three bedrooms, a bathroom, a living room, and a dining room. It had a long hall with rooms on each side, one bedroom in the front of the house and two bedrooms in the very back of the house. Each room had two large windows, a wide door, and a spacious closet. The kitchen had brown cabinets on the walls and a sink with running water. The living room, kitchen, and dining room made up one large area at the front of the house. As move-in day approached, we began to argue more and more about what room would be ours.

The house was finished in the early spring of 1969. We couldn't believe that it was finally time for us to start packing up and getting ready to relocate to our new home. We didn't have much to pack, so the packing process happened rather quickly. We didn't even need a truck. We could carry almost everything we had by hand, but Daddy got one of Mr. Bill's tractors and a trailer to move the furniture we had.

On the last day of moving our belongings into our new home, it snowed. It snowed about two inches and stopped. Snow in Sunnyside was rather unusual, so we took the fact that it snowed on that particular day as a message from God. It was God's way of purifying our home prior to us moving in. It was a testament of God's favor.

Slowly, we began getting new furniture and decorations for the new house, and over time, we'd made it into a beautiful living space.

We couldn't wait to come home from school during the cold winter season. It was a wonderful feeling knowing that we no longer had to gather firewood and chips to start a fire. We no longer had to go prime the pump for water. We enjoyed just walking into the house, flipping on a switch, and turning the lights on. The convenience of having hot and cold running water was nothing short of wonderful, and the feeling of turning a knob to warm the entire house in minutes was amazing.

It took us a while to get used to having running water. At first, everyone wanted to clean the kitchen, but our enthusiasm was short-lived. Momma ended up having to make a schedule for the chores to keep the house clean. Nothing was ever dirty, so what we were doing was preventative cleaning–cleaning before the house got dirty.

We'd use the dish detergent for a bubble bath and take long baths just to relax in our nice bathtub. Everyone took long baths except for Daddy. We'd laugh Daddy to scorn whenever he'd get out of the bathtub after just five minutes.

Not long after we moved into the new house, we were blessed with a washing machine. We still had to hang our clothes outside on the clothes lines, but at least we didn't have to wash them by hand anymore. When the clothes would finish washing, we had to take piece by piece and run it through the wringer attached to the washing machine. Soon after, we were blessed with a television set. We couldn't wait to come home from school every day to watch "Popeye the Sailor," but Momma made sure all our chores were done before we sat down to watch TV.

Though we were blessed with a TV and a washing machine, the furniture that we had in the house was limited until Denise and Anita began sending us items to fill the house. They sent us towels, pictures, window shades, and miscellaneous decorations to adorn the house. At Christmas time, we decorated every inch of our home with the decorations Denise and Anita sent.

Hedge bushes that bore beautiful flowers and lush, green grass surrounded the house. A driveway made of gravel led to the back of the house. Whenever we heard the sound of gravel crunching, we knew that someone was in our yard. There was pretty green grass that wrapped around the entire house.

* * *

We had a host of friends that couldn't wait to see our new home. They were excited for us. We had so many friends that wanted to spend the night with us, and we were delighted for them to come and share our blessing. Our parents didn't want us acting like we had been living in that brick house all our lives. So, we made sure that we were nice to everyone who came to visit.

For a long time, our house was the talk of the plantation. People made it their business to drive by just to see the new house in Sunnyside.

We couldn't wait for the school bus to pick us up. The bus would stop right in front of our house. The excitement on the bus passengers' faces looking at our home brought us excitement.

When Anita and Denise finally got the chance to visit, they were speechless. They loved the house, and they took inventory of everything we still needed to complete it. When they went back to Chicago, they sent us more items to decorate–rugs, dishes, curtains, more pictures, and bed covers.

With the decorations Anita and Denise sent, the house was finally completed. We watched our dream home built, brick by brick and our lives come together, piece by piece.

* * *

WALTER AND ROGER finished high school and went to college. They got jobs working in Mississippi. Margie and Bettina continued to go to school. Margie eventually moved to another city, but Walter, Bettina, and Roger reside in Mississippi with their families.

In January 1987, Daddy became ill while still living in the brick house in Sunnyside. He had developed cancer. So, he and mama decided to move out of the brick house to another little town in Mississippi. They wanted to live closer to Walter and Roger. Shortly after they moved, Daddy's condition began to worsen. He was eventually sent to a hospital in Jackson.

While he was in the hospital, he called Momma to his bedside and asked her for forgiveness for everything he's put her through throughout the years. She told him that everything was alright and that she had already forgiven him long ago. He told Momma that he had started seeing angels around his room. He would ask momma if she saw the angels, but she assured him that she didn't see any angels. She begged him not to leave her, but his time was nearing its end.

We all came to Jackson to be with Daddy during his final days, and we stayed right by his side until the very end.

Mama lived many years after Daddy was gone. She relocated to Greenwood again, following her Walter and Roger. She learned to enjoy living on her own, and she found new friends after joining a church.

In the summer of 2010, Momma was admitted to Greenwood Leflore Hospital for what **we** thought was a case of dehydration and stomach pain. We always knew that she suffered from rheumatoid arthritis, but we had no idea that our mom would never come home again. As time went by, her health began declining. It seemed as though Momma was being diagnosed with a new sickness every week. We decided to transfer her to a hospital in Jackson, Mississippi.

We were right there with Momma as much as possible, crying and praying. We did everything we could to try to hold ourselves together, but our strength was wearing thin.

Momma fought hard and held on as long as she could. We kept praying for change, but God's plan was different than our own. Momma never recovered from her illness, and after a few months in the hospital, she passed away.

Mama was our rock. To lose her was beyond devastating. To have lost both of our parents felt unreal. They both passed away within months of being admitted into the hospital, which I counted as a blessing. They didn't have to suffer long.

Even though Momma and Daddy left us unexpectedly, we were grateful to God for allowing us the time that we did get to spend with them.

By the grace of God, my six siblings and I are still alive.

* * *

We always go back to visit Sunnyside whenever we go home to see family. The Gin Lott where we once lived is nothing more than a wasteland now, and the brick house is always occupied. Farming is not as popular as it was, and some farmers decided to turn some areas of their farms into catfish ponds. The houses that used to make up Sunnyside are now gone, and much of the land is desolate farmland.

Whenever we go back home, it's a joy to ride out to Sunnyside to look at what was once our home. Even though the houses and the people that once made Sunnyside a vibrant and bustling community are gone, we enjoy the nostalgia that we get simply being in Sunnyside. Regardless of where or how far we go, Sunnyside will always be home for us.

ACKNOWLEDGMENTS

My heartfelt thanks to everyone especially my family who delightfully allowed, encouraged, and helped me along the way in telling my story. I want to thank my wonderful husband Arlee for being so supportive and for standing by me during this long and difficult journey. I'd like to thank my children-Arlee III and Konesha for all their hard work and expertise in helping me. Many times they were forced to read my book and to make corrections; but they did it with much love. Special thanks to my awesome god daughter Doricia who sticks by my side in all my endeavors; I am so honored and blessed to have you in my life.

I thank God for my siblings for allowing me to tell their stories especially Roger with his astounding memories. Being the youngest sibling in our family he shared information that was long forgotten. I remember talking to him one day concerning my feelings about telling our story. I never will forget what he said to me, he told me to just tell the truth and not hold back and everything else will fall in place. That motivated me more than anything and that's exactly what I did in writing our memoir.

Special thanks to Denise our oldest sister for all the help she gave me; for countless days and hours she spent on the phone refreshing my mind of many childhood memories. To all of my siblings, thank each of you for refreshing my memories with the many events and stories you shared along the way. There were so many wonderful and great pieces of our pass that each of you brought to my remembrance. In all honesty, our memoir would not be the same without your help.

Thanks to all my many family members and friends for your encouragement, love, prayers and support. My sincere thanks to Mrs. Connie Hogan, an awesome and special friend being 92 years old. She was so amazing and helpful in encouraging and correcting me in the beginning stages of my book. She will always be a part of me and remembered for all her wisdom and knowledge. She has since gone on to be with the Lord. Special thanks to her daughter Kathy Cunningham for reaching out to me in countless ways, your love and kindness will always be remembered.

I want to say to you, never think for a moment that you are incapable of pursuing your goals and dreams. I believe everyone has a goal, whether it is long term or short term. First, you must believe in yourself and your ability to achieve whatever it is you desire. Second, do not be a quitter; the lesser your chances look, the harder you must work to give it your all.

I strongly believe that striving and struggles precede success. Most of all, put God first in all your doings and watch him show up and show out for you.

ORA TANNER-MARTIN

CPSIA information can be obtained
at www.ICGtesting.com
Printed in the USA
FSHW010033120521
81231FS

9 780578 798080